I0817818

THE HOLIDAY BOYFRIEND

CHRISTINA BENJAMIN

Published in the United States by Crown Atlantic Publishing

ISBN 978-1-7326123-3-4

Text set in Adobe Garamond

Version 1.1
Printed in the United States of America
First edition hardcover printed, November 2018

To those who choose to believe in the magic of Christmas and never give up on miracles.

PROLOGUE

A Haute Chic's Holiday Survival Guide

1. *Family drama is much easier to face with fierce lips.*
2. *Manolos are as last season as mistletoe.*
3. . . .

Emma Rhodes stared at the blinking cursor on her laptop. She needed a third bullet point for her fashion blog, *Fifth Ave Fab – A Haute Chic's Guide to Life,* but nothing was coming to her. She popped another wintermint Tic Tac into her mouth, crushing it in frustration. She looked at the empty candy container. *Damn.* She'd gone through a whole pack already.

Sighing, Emma turned back to her laptop. She needed to wrap up her latest entry. She'd promised her guidance counselor she'd have it ready to add to her portfolio by the time she returned from winter break.

Emma was perhaps the last high school senior at Stanton Prep to not submit her college applications. It's not that she didn't know what she wanted to do. She'd known she was going to go to school for fashion since she was old enough to spell Versace. And until last year, Emma would've said she was only applying to her dream school, Parsons, in New York City.

But twelve months ago, Emma found herself fleeing to Boston with her mother after divorce and deception had rocked her perfect Manhattan existence. And now, with only one term of high school looming between Emma and her future, she had a big decision to make.

Boston or New York? Her mother or her father? Boston University or Parsons School of Design? Flee for a fresh start or face old wounds?

Emma stared at her laptop, the cursor taunting her. Writing witty commentary on her blog had been her outlet since she left New York, and it normally came easy to her. But as her train chugged steadily toward Manhattan, she couldn't concentrate. Perhaps she was more nervous about her first trip home than she'd thought. After all, she'd left the city for a reason—*a tall, dark and handsome reason.*

Emma sighed, trying to expel her jitters. She'd been looking forward to going home for the holidays for months. This would be the first Christmas she got to spend with her father since the divorce, and she wasn't going to let anyone keep her from enjoying it. Especially not a particularly gorgeous blue-eyed boy with a devastating smile. For all Emma cared, Will Taylor's chestnuts could be roasting on an open fire. She was going to explore her collegiate options and enjoy her holiday homecoming. Besides, nobody did Christmas like Manhattan.

1

Emma

EMMA KNOCKED on the door again, louder this time. But still there was no answer. "Great. Just great," she muttered. One Christmas in Boston and her father had forgotten about her. Emma heard the bitter words of her mother echoed in her subconscious. '*He's replaced us.*' Emma shuddered against the classic divorce cliché. She knew marriages fell apart, but parents didn't replace their kids. Surely Emma's father hadn't replaced her. She'd always been his princess—a daddy's girl to the core.

She knocked one more time before slumping to the floor. Leaning against the door, Emma released a frustrated breath. *Where the hell was her father?* They were supposed to spend Christmas break together, and Emma had been looking forward to it for months. Her last Christmas was awful. Her mother hadn't even let the ink dry on her divorce settlement before hauling Emma to Boston, where they spent the holiday eating Chinese food in a cold, empty brownstone.

Emma hated everything about Boston. She got that her mother needed a fresh start, and if she were being honest, Emma had wanted one too. But trading Manhattan for Boston was a like going from couture to off-the-rack—depressing.

Emma's parents were well known in the elite Manhattan social circles and their divorce had been a very public and nasty one when word of her father's mistress got out. Even the students at Emma's prep school, the prestigious St. James Academy, were whispering about her father's affair with some gold-digging model from South Carolina. But that's not why Emma had been eager to flee. She was running from a broken heart of her own, caused by her ex-best friend and debilitating crush, Will Taylor.

Emma was grateful when the ding of the elevator distracted her from her spiraling thoughts of Christmas past. She looked down the hall of the posh high-rise apartment sure she'd see her father rushing toward her, an apology gift in hand for his tardiness. But it was only a well-dressed elderly couple. Emma sighed, sinking further into her spot on the floor. She shrugged off her red Burberry peacoat and pulled her iPhone from her Louis Vuitton hoping for a Christmas miracle, but it was still dead, just like it had been thirty minutes ago. She'd been watching movies on the train from Boston and killed the battery. And of course, she'd forgotten to pack a charger.

Tapping her foot restlessly, Emma racked her brain trying to remember if she knew anyone that lived in this building. Her father had sold their palatial penthouse apartment right after he divorced her mother, claiming he could no longer afford it after, "the God damned settlement your mother clawed out of me." Emma knew that wasn't true. Her father was a Wall Street legend. He owned a rather prestigious investment firm and according to the press, was doing just fine. She figured the change of scenery was because he'd wanted a fresh start too. Emma wished he could have just admitted that. It would've made losing her childhood home a bit easier.

Emma used to be close to her father, but since the divorce they'd grown apart. This would be the first time she saw his new place. She'd wanted to come back over spring break, but her father said he was in the middle of moving. Then over summer break, his excuse was he'd just started dating someone and thought it was, "too soon," to introduce her to Emma. *Although, is there ever a good time to meet the woman wearing your mother's Louboutins?*

Emma hated thinking about her father's new girlfriend, but the mystery woman seemed to keep finding a way into her thoughts. Especially now that Emma was back in New York. She was used to being the center of her father's attention—learning to share the spotlight might be more difficult than she'd imagined. Particularly because Emma couldn't help wondering if the other woman was the reason why her father was currently standing her up. *Was he out wining and dining his new girlfriend somewhere? Or worse, were they in the middle of some romantic liaison?*

Emma pressed her palms into her eyelids until she saw spots. She did *not* want to think about her father and some other woman. *Gross!* Old people romance gave Emma the creeps. Her father was fifty-seven. He was supposed to be collecting expensive cars, not notches on his bedpost.

The elevator dinged again. Emma didn't bother looking up this time. It was probably just another stuffy old Manhattan couple. She closed her eyes and pretended to be sleeping to spare herself the pity from whoever walked by. Because no matter how fabulous Emma was dressed, there was no way to make looking abandoned before the holidays seem in style.

"Well, well. Looks like Christmas came early this year."

Emma's eyes flew open. She'd know that voice anywhere. And when she looked up, her heart stopped. There he was, staring at her with that irresistible smile and looking as alarmingly good-looking as she'd remembered—Will Taylor.

2

ill

WILL PRACTICALLY STUMBLED when he saw Emma Rhodes sitting in the hall of his luxury apartment building. He pushed his thick dark hair back from his eyes, blinking twice to make sure he wasn't hallucinating. But there she was, as gorgeous as ever in Gucci and lip gloss. It was all very ghost of Christmas past, and Will shuddered at the painful longing she evoked. *How many times had he dreamt of this moment in the past year?* Too many.

Thankfully, Emma's eyes were closed, giving Will a minute to collect himself. Although, as usual, he hadn't really used the time to his advantage. He'd wanted to say, "You're back. I've missed you. How are you? What are you doing here?" Any number of those things would've been better than what came out of his mouth. "Well, well. Looks like Christmas came early this year."

Emma's vivid green eyes snapped open at the sound of his voice. Will watched shock flare across her features, before it simmered into something like resentment. Will knew it was petty but he didn't care. Emma had hurt him like no other girl had, and apparently his heart wasn't ready to forgive her—regardless of it being the holiday season.

"Will?" she asked, staring at him like she'd seen a ghost. And sort of like she'd rather be anywhere else in the world right now. *Good*. Emma should feel bad. She stood him up at the winter formal last year. Will had stood outside the Plaza holding her stupid corsage for an hour waiting for her to show up. He'd looked like a total loser. He ended up going in with Liz Vanderveer and getting drunk on peppermint schnapps.

"What are you doing here?" Emma asked scrambling to her feet.

Will's scorned heart hijacked his brain and snark poured out of his mouth before he could stop himself. "Not that I owe you an explanation, but I live here."

Emma crossed her arms. "Since when?"

"Since when do you care?" he countered.

She blew out a breath. "I guess I don't. I'm just here to spend Christmas with my father."

Will stuffed his hands in his pockets, giving Emma a snide smile. "Looks like a fun reunion."

Ever since Theodore Rhodes moved into the apartment next door to Will's, he'd been waiting for Emma to come visit. But now that she was here, he was tongue-tied by the dormant hurt that smoldered in his heart.

"Are you sure you were expected?" he asked nodding to the nest of designer accessories and luggage on the floor. "You do have a reputation for not showing."

Emma glared at him. "He's just running a bit late."

Will scoffed. "Ya know, that's what I told myself at the formal last year."

"Excuse me?" Emma asked arching her pale eyebrows.

"Whatever," Will mumbled starting to walk away. He didn't feel like dredging up old wounds in a hallway for anyone to overhear, but Emma called after him.

"Will, wait."

He turned around and the pleading look on Emma's face hit him like a punch to the gut. *Shit. Why couldn't he get over her?*

"About last year . . ." she started. But something kept her from saying more, and suddenly Will didn't think he could handle hearing more.

"Forget it," he mumbled. "And don't worry about your father. He probably just took Hodor for a walk. I'm sure they'll be back soon."

"Hodor?" Emma asked, confusion pinching her delicate features.

"Yeah. Colin's dog."

"Who's Colin?"

"Tara's son."

Emma's pretty face paled and her mouth hung open in a perfect O. That was not the face of someone who knew her father was living with his mistress and her son. *Nice work, Will.*

Emma took a step toward him, her familiar scent of vanilla sugar cookies invading his space. Emma's vibrant green eyes sparkled furiously like slivers of cut emerald. "Tara? As in the Tara that broke up my parents' marriage?" she asked blinking rapidly. "Does that sheet serpent live here?"

"Uh . . ." Will's mind went blank. Being so close to Emma made it impossible to speak. She was stunning. Her long ash-blonde hair hung in soft waves over her shoulders as she moved toward Will. And despite her fury, all Will could presently think of doing was running his hands through it. He stared at Emma's lips. They were perfectly glossed in pale pink. She pursed them in annoyance and he was instantly reminded of the pale pink rose buds in the corsage he'd bought her last year. His heart twisted and he took a step back. "I don't know, Em. I'm not his secretary."

Emma looked crestfallen. She bit her lip, crossing her arms. "That's great. Just freaking great! I can't believe this." She turned away from Will and started pacing in front of her father's door, muttering to herself. "My first time home . . . He doesn't even have the decency to show up . . . He's probably with *her!* He never let *me* get a dog! I guess I'm doomed to have terrible holidays from now on."

Will watched Emma's mini-meltdown in silent fascination until she started to gather her things. "Where are you going?"

"Home," she muttered.

Will caught her arm as she tried to push past him. "You are home."

"I meant Boston."

"New York is home, Em."

"Yeah, well it certainly doesn't feel like it."

"Look, why don't you come to my place to wait for your father? My parents aren't home and—"

Emma interrupted him with a shrill laugh. "I'm sorry. Are you seriously hitting on me right now?"

"What? No!"

"Oh really? The whole, my parents aren't home routine? Good to see not everything has changed. You're still the same old Will."

"What's that supposed to mean?"

The elevator dinged and they both turned to see Emma's father step out, one arm around a gorgeous brunette, the other holding the mittened hand of a rosy-cheeked little boy. Will's hand was still on Emma's arm and he felt her go rigid.

"Emma!" her father greeted. "What are you doing here?"

3

Emma

IF EMMA WERE MADE of glass she would've shattered right there on the spot. Seeing the picturesque family scene unfolding in the elevator had stolen her breath. But when her father looked at her with a mixture of confusion and surprise, her heart broke. He'd truly forgotten about her—and she could see why. He was attached at the hip to a woman who looked like she could be Cindy Crawford's younger sister. *Much, much younger sister*.

The woman who'd stolen her father certainly wasn't the old maid Emma had been imagining. She probably wasn't even thirty. And the apple-cheeked little boy getting sloppy dog kisses from the regal-looking golden retriever only added to the perfect family portrait—one that Emma was definitely no longer a part of.

The little boy looked at Emma as soon as her father called

her by name. His blue eyes brightened and he pushed his pale, snow-covered hair from his eyes. "You're Emma? You're gonna be my sister!"

The super model spoke, corralling the little boy and his dog before he could make his way toward Emma. "Honey, remember what we said about grown up talk? Let's let Teddy speak to Emma first."

Teddy? Did that woman just call her father, Teddy? As in a cute, cuddly stuffed bear? Emma's father was Theodore Rhodes, world-renowned Wall Street mogul. No one called him Teddy.

"Emma, I'm glad you're here," her father announced.

"I've been here, Dad. For like an hour. Did you forget about me?"

"No . . . " He glanced at the super model. They exchanged secret smiles. "It's been a bit exciting around here lately. I just lost track of time. But come inside, we have a lot to talk about."

"Clearly," Emma muttered under her breath.

"I guess I'll see you later?" Will called, startling Emma.

She'd forgotten he was still standing there. She watched him walk away, leaving her to follow her father and his strange replacement family into the apartment. Emma took a deep breath, grabbing her things. She stared up and down the empty hallway of the posh Manhattan apartment building, wondering when New York had changed so much.

4

ill

Once inside his apartment, Will leaned against the door. He couldn't believe Emma was actually here. Her soft vanilla fragrance still invaded his senses as he replayed their conversation over and over in his mind. *Why did he have to come off so arrogant and sleazy when he was nervous?*

He hadn't meant to hit on her. At least he didn't think he had. But he couldn't deny he still had some sort of feelings for her. Call it unrequited love, but there was unfinished business between them, and Will wouldn't be able to get Emma out of his head until he got to the bottom of it.

He needed to figure out a way to see her again. He thought for a minute and pulled out his phone, selecting a contact under favorites and banging out a text.

Will: Hey Cran, feel like throwing a party?
Cranston: What's the occasion?
Will: When have you ever needed one?
Cranston: Touché

WILL CRACKED A SMILE, practically able to hear Cranston's preppy drawl.

Will: Tomorrow night. The hotel.
Cranston: Done. Guest list? The usual suspects?
Will: Actually, I need you to invite our whole class.
Cranston: This just got interesting. Do tell, William.

WILL COULD PICTURE Cranston's look of amusement. He didn't normally mingle with the '*little people,*' as he called them. But then again when your father owned one of the biggest hotels in Manhattan, everyone was the '*little people*.' But Cranston liked to think of himself as the Gatsby of St. James, so slumming it sometimes appealed to the philanthropist in him.

Will: I'll explain later.
Cranston: You bet your ass you will, but my priorities are on the ladies. Any special requests?
Will: Nah. I got my date covered.

OR HE WOULD RATHER, if Emma accepted.

Cranston: Nice. I'm feeling a martinis and mistletoe vibe. You down?
Will: Sure, whatever you want. Just send out the blast.
Cranston: On it.

WILL SLIPPED his phone into his pocket and let the utter silence of his empty apartment wash over him. He looked around the massive space with disgust, still bitter his parents had uprooted him to move to the giant flat six months ago. In Will's opinion it was a total waste. The Upper East Side was all the same to him. Who cared that they moved two buildings closer to Central Park and had a few more square feet? They certainly didn't need the extra space.

It was just Will and his parents who lived there. Although, *lived*, was quite a loose term considering his parents were away more than they were home. Will was closer to the full-time staff that cared for the palatial apartment than he was to his parents these days.

He was the youngest of five boys, with a six-year gap between his closest brother, Gabe. Once Gabe graduated and shipped off to college, Will's parents started traveling. Each year the trips grew longer. This year, they'd hardly been home at all. He knew they didn't need to. Will's mother didn't work and his father owned an international software company that allowed him to work from anywhere. But Will couldn't help feeling slighted. It's not that he needed looking after, but it was his last year of high school. It would've been nice if his parents at least pretended to care, like they had with his brothers.

Will sighed, wagering whether his parents would make it home for Christmas. Just the other day, Sharon, his favorite housekeeper, had asked him if he wanted a Christmas tree delivered in case his parents were held up. Sharon had been with Will's family since before he was born. She was like a sudo-mom to him. And although he knew Sharon was only looking out for him, Will had stubbornly declined her Christmas tree offer.

Picking out their holiday tree was the one tradition his family had. Every year, they drove to a little tree farm upstate and picked out the perfect Christmas tree. They cut it down and everything. He knew he shouldn't hold his breath, but Will wasn't quite ready to let go of the last of his childhood just yet.

5

Emma

EMMA'S JAW dropped when she walked into her father's new apartment. Everything was white and silver, polished to a near blinding glare. The style was so modern it made the Museum of Modern Art look outdated. Emma was afraid to touch anything. Her heart ached for their old home. It had been cozy and warm, full of buttery leather sofas, crackling fireplaces and thick rugs you could curl up on. This place was cold, and the white marble floor reflected the feeling.

The other thing that struck her as odd was the size of the apartment. It's not that it was small. The living room, kitchen and dining room were more than spacious, and the floor-to-ceiling windows gave an impressive view of the Upper East Side. But their old apartment had been larger. Eight bedrooms larger—as if her parents had had plans to one day fill the empty rooms with brothers and sisters for Emma. Instead, they'd filled the space with enough betrayal and resentment to cost her a lifetime of therapy.

"Emma!" The cherub-cheeked little boy tugged on her sleeve. "Do you wanna see my room?"

"Your room?" *Did he live here?*

"Colin, honey, why don't we take Hodor to your room and let Emma settle in."

The dog's name finally registered with Emma. Hodor . . . as in *'Game of Thrones.' Did that mean the pint-sized progeny watched the violent HBO saga?* He couldn't be more than seven or eight. If that were the case, Tara wouldn't be winning Mother of the Year anytime soon. She should probably start saving for therapy now.

Emma watched as Tara guided Colin and presumably, Hodor, away, leaving Emma alone with her father at last. She did a quick scan of the apartment. Only three doors led off the hallway. She assumed one was a bathroom, and that meant . . .

"Darling," her father called from the wet bar where he was mixing a fru-fru looking vodka drink. *Since when did he drink vodka?* Her father drank scotch, neat. Maybe it was for Tara. It looked like something a wannabe super model would drink.

"I have some exciting news," her father said, startling Emma back to reality—*if that's what this was.*

"More exciting than your new love of the absence of color?" she asked gesturing to the blank apartment walls as she plugged in her phone to charge.

He chuckled like she was joking, then took a sip of the pink drink. *So not for the mistress, then?*

Emma watched as he sighed and rubbed his forehead. "This isn't how I'd hoped to break the news to you."

"What news?"

"Tara and I are getting married."

"What?" Emma's voice was barely a whisper, but her father held up a hand.

"And we're expecting."

"Expecting what?" *A lobotomy, an alien invasion, the apocalypse?*

Aside from those reasons, why the hell would Emma's father be marrying his mistress? The woman who ruined their lives!

"Expecting a child," he clarified with finality.

Emma blinked rapidly, trying to wake from the nightmare she was trapped in. It was an effort to stay on her feet.

"I hope I can count on you to be mature about this, Emma. It's a joyous occasion and I'd like you to be a part of it."

"A joyous occasion? Are you joking?"

"Not at all. I've always wanted more children."

"And what, Mom couldn't give them to you so you traded her in for a hot pair of birthing hips?"

"Emma—"

"What? It's the truth, isn't it?"

"That's enough," her father bellowed. "I expect you to be respectful of Tara and her son. They're part of our family now."

"What family?" Emma hissed.

"Em . . ." Her father took a step toward her but she backed away.

"Just tell me one thing, Dad. Do I still have a room here with our *new family*?"

His tired sigh was all the confirmation she needed.

"That's what I thought." She grabbed her coat and stormed out of the apartment. *So much for coming back to New York!*

6

ill

Will stood outside Emma's door trying to figure out how to invite her to the impromptu party he'd forced Cranston to throw. It was the only reason he could come up with for seeing her again. He couldn't just ask her out after a year without speaking. That would seem desperate. Not to mention how badly he'd botched their encounter in the hall earlier.

He was still stalling, perfecting his casual look when Emma came barreling through the door and slammed into his chest. His arms instinctively steadied her, wrapping around her waist. She yelped in surprise and looked up at him. That's when he noticed the tears in her eyes.

"Hey, are you okay?" Will asked.

"Obviously not!" she yelled, pushing him away.

Will caught her hand and pulled her back. "Em, what's wrong?"

"Like you care." She shook his grasp and ran to the elevator, frantically pushing the down button.

"Maybe I do," he blurted when he caught up to her.

Emma turned, flooring him with her stunning green eyes. She looked furious, but the quiver in her pink lips told him her tears were about to get worse. *No, no, no! Not good!* Will couldn't handle crying girls. It was his kryptonite. And anytime he witnessed it he found himself promising anything to make them stop. One time he'd promised his little cousin he'd buy her a pony!

Hoping to avoid being sucked into Emma's helpless blubbering, Will pulled her into a hug. *Perhaps not the best move.* Touching Emma might actually be worse than seeing her cry, which from the shaking of her shoulders, Will was sure she was doing anyway.

He ran a soothing hand over her glossy blonde hair, filling the hall with her intoxicating vanilla fragrance. *The girl smelled like a damn Christmas cookie.* It was irresistible.

"How 'bout we go get some hot chocolate and talk about it?" Will offered.

Emma looked up, her watery green eyes making his heart stutter. "Jacques?" she asked, sounding slightly hopeful.

Jacques Torres Chocolate was Emma's favorite. She and Will used to go there to do their homework after school when they were barely teenagers. They would cut through Central Park and Will shot films along the way, each time claiming the current reel was his *'best yet'.*

Will had thousands of hours of Emma twirling through Central Park, posing on benches, kicking through piles of leaves and clutching hot chocolate in her mittened hands. The mere mention of Jacques brought all those memories rushing back to him. He'd been kidding himself thinking he was over Emma. As he stared into her dazzling eyes, he realized that would be like getting over the stars—*impossible.*

"Where else?" Will replied, softly.

The elevator dinged and the door finally opened. Will extended his arm and Emma took it. And suddenly, it was as if she'd never left.

7

Emma

EMMA FORGOT how nice it was to have someone to talk to. Will sat across from her in their usual spot at Jacques Torres. Eli, the barista still worked there and he even remembered Emma, right down to her preference for smoked sea salt, orange zest and marshmallows in her cocoa.

Sipping her favorite concoction across from Will made Emma's heart skip a beat. His gorgeous smile was so familiar it tugged at the old ache she'd been trying to bury. And for the first time since she'd come back to New York, Emma felt like she was home.

"So," Will said. "Is it really that bad?"

"What?"

"Your father's new place? I just figured that's what you were upset about."

Emma laughed. "Actually, yeah. It's pretty awful. I don't even have my own room. Can you believe that?"

"Harsh. Where are you supposed to sleep?"

Emma slouched at the prospects. "I don't know. The couch?"

"Well, my offer still stands." Will held his hands up before she could sneer at him. "Let me clarify. My purely innocent offer still stands. My brothers haven't been home in years and my folks are out of town as usual, so there's plenty of empty bedrooms at my place if you get tired of the couch."

"Thanks. I may take you up on it," she replied, thinking of the uncomfortable-looking white slab that her father was trying to pass off as a couch. "When did you move by the way?"

Will waved his hand dismissively. "A few months ago. Sore subject."

Emma nodded, understanding completely.

"So tell me something good," Will said, changing the subject. "How's school?"

Emma groaned. "Sore Subject."

"Really? I thought you were loving it in Boston."

That's what Emma had told her best friend Kensie Davenport. Kensie was the only person Emma kept in contact with from her old school. And if Will knew Emma was boasting that Boston was great . . . *Did that mean he was asking about her?*

She rubbed her temples then took another sip of hot chocolate. Emma was never good at the mind games and social politics that went along with trying to figure out if guys were into her. She liked to be straightforward. And based on what her parents had gone through, Emma was convinced it was the best policy.

"Yeah, I don't know why I said that. I hate Boston."

"Why?"

"I don't know. It's not New York."

"That's it?" Will asked. "Seems cruel to hate on a city for not being New York. I mean by that logic all cities suck." Will's eyes twinkled like ice chips as he recited one of his favorite quotes. "You haven't lived until you've died in New York," he said with bravado.

She laughed. It was so good to be around someone who got it. New York City was the best place in the world. And not many people had experienced the city like Emma had, but Will was one of the few. Growing up in Manhattan, going to elite prep schools, having a doorman, car service and private shopping accounts at Barney's . . . It was amazing. But all of it disappeared when Emma moved to Boston.

It wasn't just the posh lifestyle she missed. Emma missed New York. The electric buzz that seemed to breathe life into the thriving metropolis. The eclectic melting pot of food and style. The constant movement of music and art. New York was alive. And that pulse was what Emma missed most. *Well that, and her family.*

For as long as she could remember, she wanted to study fashion, and New York was the mecca for that. Lately, her mother had tried to convince Emma that Boston had style too, but so far she hadn't seen anything she liked. Especially not at her stuffy new school, Stanton Prep.

"It's not just that Boston isn't New York," Emma complained. "I sorta hate my new school, too."

"You're going to Stanton, right?"

Emma nodded and took another sip of her cocoa trying to hide her surprise. *How did Will know so much about her?* He said it so casually she wondered if maybe it was something everyone knew. Rumors did circulate around her old school like wildfire. Maybe she was reading too much into Will's knowledge.

"I heard Stanton's a great school," Will added.

"It is, but most of the kids there suck."

"Why?"

"They think they're beyond superior. Which is ridiculous considering half of them haven't ever been to New York City."

"The nerve!" Will teased.

Emma swatted him.

"So you're seriously telling me you don't rule that school by now?"

"Not even close. There's this group of rich snobs there and get this, they call themselves the *Goldens*."

"You're kidding?"

"I wish."

Will's eyes sparkled with mischief. "I could totally make a movie about this."

Emma laughed. "You sound like Megan."

"Megan?"

"She's a film student and like the only cool person I've met."

"I like her already. Tell me more."

"There's not much to tell. Her best friend moved to Ireland, so Megan sorta took me in. But besides with her, I just don't feel like I can fit in there."

Will reached across the table and squeezed her hand. "That doesn't sound like the Emma I remember. She could do anything."

Emotion pressed at the back of Emma's throat. She hadn't felt like that Emma in a long time. "I miss that Emma."

"We all do."

She looked up. "What?"

"Well, most of us. Marcy Foy and Liz Vanderveer are still battling to fill your shoes as queen bee of the hive, but St. James isn't the same without you."

"God, I haven't heard those names in a while." Emma hesitated, but she had to ask, if only to protect herself from a repeat of last year. "Are you and Liz together?"

Will nearly choked on his cocoa. "What? Liz? God no!"

Emma released the breath she hadn't realized she was

holding.

"I've missed you, Em." Will squeezed her hand again. "All of us have. And that's why you should come to the party tomorrow."

"What party?"

"Cranston's throwing an end of term party at the hotel tomorrow night. The whole class is invited. I know everyone would love to see you."

"Oh," Emma's eyes flicked away from the intensity in Will's. "I guess that would be fun. But I haven't even told anyone I was back in town."

"Not even Kensie?"

"No. I was sorta planning on just spending time with my father, but since that's not gonna happen . . ."

"It sounds like you're in need of some New York fun. We can go to Cranston's together if you want?"

Emma shrugged and against her better judgment, blurted, "Okay."

Will grinned. "It's a date."

Emma let her heart flutter hesitantly. Will had always been charming, and that was half the trouble. Every girl at St. James would let his grin charm them right out of their plaid skirts.

But Emma decided she would try to keep the past in the past. She needed to see if she could handle being back in New York. So far, Will wasn't acting like the horny boy who broke her heart. Actually, he seemed more like the Will she'd grown up with. The one she'd been friends with and spent years pining for. He was certainly being more thoughtful and chivalrous than she remembered.

He'd been genuinely kind to her since he'd found her rushing teary-eyed from her father's apartment. She decided to give him the benefit of the doubt. Emma had changed in the year she'd spent in Boston, and she found herself wondering if maybe Will had changed too.

8

ill

Will was pleased with himself as he walked Emma back to their apartment building. *Mission accomplished.* Emma was his date for tomorrow's party. He'd finally have a chance to see if there was something between them or put his feelings to rest once and for all. Although, after their hot cocoa date, he was positive there was still something there. He'd felt that spark that always sizzled around him when he was with Emma. After all this time it hadn't faded. Even when Emma had left him with only heartache and confusion.

Will still couldn't figure out why Emma had left the way she had. They'd been friends since third grade. They'd practically grown up together. And Will didn't know when things had changed, but somewhere between algebra and hot cocoa he'd fallen in love with her. Of course he never had the courage to admit it. He was terrified it would ruin their friendship. Especially since Emma had never given him any signs that she felt the same way.

The closest Will had come to admitting his feelings was when he'd asked Emma to their winter formal last year. And even then, the credit for his rare act of bravery belonged mostly to Cranston's flask of whiskey. But that liquid courage-fueled moment had been the first time Will thought maybe, just maybe, he had a chance for something more than friendship with his dream girl.

Being with Emma today had brought all those old feelings rushing back. But the pain of their foiled formal came back with it. He was itching to ask her what happened that night and finally get some clarity, but things were going so well and he didn't want to ruin it.

As they walked through the park in comfortable silence, Will found himself wondering if maybe bringing Emma to Cranston's party wasn't such a good idea. He and Emma had always been good one-on-one. It was when their friends got involved that things seemed to get messed up.

The silence grew uncomfortable when Will found himself alone in the elevator with Emma. He didn't know why, but elevators always had a special ability to magnify awkwardness. And to make matters worse, someone had added a bough of mistletoe in the tastefully decorated car. Will cleared his throat when he noticed it, drawing Emma's attention.

He watched her cheeks blush when she saw what he was staring at. She started to step away from him, but Will caught her hand. "Em, I didn't mean it like that. That is, unless you wanted me to?"

Emma gave him a shy grin, filling Will with unusual courage. He took a step closer. Then another, until they were standing inches apart, directly under the mistletoe.

"Today's been fun," he murmured. "I'm really glad I ran into you."

"Me too."

"I meant what I said, Em. I've missed you. And if you need a place to stay while you're in town, my door is always open. Plus, it'd be nice to get to spend some more time together."

"I think I'd like that," Emma whispered.

Will moved closer. "Me too."

He brushed a strand of silky blonde hair away from Emma's pale cheek. His hand stayed there, gently holding her face. Will stared into her wide green eyes, his heart hammering in his chest. This was it. The moment he'd imagined a million times in his head. He was seconds away from kissing Emma.

She closed her eyes and Will took a deep breath, trying to keep his hands from trembling as he pulled her closer. He tilted her delicate jaw angling it toward him. Their noses met and he felt the intake of breath as Emma's lips parted, mere inches from claiming his. The elevator dinged and the doors began to part. Will hadn't even noticed they'd stopped moving. Perhaps that was because the entire world had ceased to exist with Emma's lips so close to his. *Do it, Will. Now's your chance, just kiss her, damn it.*

But as the doors opened, the spell they were under began to dissolve. Will opened his eyes and nearly stumbled back in shock at the girl standing on his floor. "Liz?"

9

Emma

EMMA'S EYES flew open and she took a step back from Will. "No, actually my name's Emma." She scathed. "Is it really that hard to remember the name of the girls you invite to your apartment? Or was she just the last skank you brought here?"

"Guilty," chirped a shrill voice, sending chills down Emma's spine. She turned to see none other than Liz Vanderveer standing just outside the elevator, smirking like the Grinch who stole Christmas.

"Hey Emmy, so good to see you," Liz crooned, a saccharine smile plastered across her flawless red lips.

"Hey Lizzy," Emma replied, equally fake.

Liz didn't even give her a second glance. Instead she zeroed in on Will. "Will, darling, I'm so glad I finally caught you. Did you forget I was coming over?"

Will just stood speechless in the elevator until the doors

began to close. Emma reached out to stop them, pushing past him into the hall. Suddenly, it seemed entirely too crowded with Liz standing between them. Intimate images of Liz and Will popped in Emma's mind like flashbulbs, bringing back all the pain and embarrassment she thought she'd left behind. Liz flashed a grin like she knew exactly what Emma was thinking, and looped her arm through Will's as if marking her territory.

Liz gazed up at Will, blinking her dark doe eyes. "Don't worry, I used my key," she said, proffering a shiny brass key that obviously belonged to Will's apartment. "And I spoke to your mother earlier. She said they've been delayed and won't be back until Christmas Eve. But don't worry, I told her I'd stick around and keep you company."

Emma felt her stomach lurch. She needed to get the hell away from Liz before she said something she'd regret.

"Come on," Liz purred, tugging on Will's arm. "I ordered in from, Jean-Georges. It should be here any minute."

Emma didn't even try to hide her snort of disgust and she stomped down the hall. *Will hadn't changed at all.*

He called after her. "Emma, wait."

"For what, Will? Looks like your apartment isn't so lonely after all."

Then she disappeared into her father's apartment, slamming the door in his face.

The trouble with not having her own room after having her heart stomped on was that there wasn't anywhere Emma could go to breakdown. And that's exactly what she was on the verge of. All she wanted was a pint of Ben & Jerry's and a bedroom to hide in. She decided to text Kensie. Maybe she could just hideout at her best friend's house and binge cheesy Christmas movies until this nightmare of a holiday was over.

Emma retrieved her phone from where she'd left it charging in the kitchen. She unplugged it and tapped out a text to Kensie.

Emma: SOS. Can I come over?
Kensie: To my house? Where are you?
Emma: NYC. My father's place. It's a disaster.
Kensie: Are you joking?
Emma: Nope. I'm desperate. I need a place to crash.
Kensie: I'm in France!

Emma let out a tiny sob and squeezed her eyes shut. *Of course Kensie was in France.* She went skiing in the French Alps with her family every year over winter break. If Emma hadn't been such an absentee friend she would've remembered that. *Maybe this was what she deserved?* Emma had lost touch with everyone from New York, even her best friend. It had been stupid to think she could just come back and pick up where she left off.

Kensie: Emma is everything okay?
Emma: Yeah. It's nothing. Just family drama.
Kensie: I'm sorry, Em. I wish I was there. I miss you.
Emma: I miss you, too. Have fun in France.

Emma turned her phone off and slipped it into her pocket, deciding to scour the freezer. *Pregnant people liked ice cream didn't they?* Ice cream was the only thing that could salvage Emma's wreck of a day. She didn't have her best friend or a room to hide it, but if she could just find some damn ice cream . . . But when she searched the freezer's contents and came up empty, Emma's mood only worsened. "No, of course that was too much to ask," she muttered to herself. "Why would the home wrecker keep ice cream on hand?" she groaned, her head still half in the freezer.

"What's a home wrecker?" asked a squeaky voice.

Emma slammed the freezer shut to see Colin and his giant retriever standing in the kitchen. "Oh, hey. I didn't see you there."

He grinned. "I saw you. What's a home wrecker?"

Shit, this kid wasn't gonna let it go. "I'll tell you when you're older."

"I'm seven and Mom says I'm old for my age," Colin snapped back.

"Yeah, old enough to watch Game of Thrones, apparently," Emma muttered to herself, trying to push past Hodor who was eyeing her with distrust.

A huge smile lit Colin's face. "Game of Thrones is my favorite show in the whole world! How did you know that?"

Emma shrugged. "Your dog's name is Hodor."

"His full name is Hodor Targaryen," Colin replied proudly.

Emma cocked her head to the side. As a huge fan of the show, she couldn't let that go. "Um, you know Hodor's not a Targaryen, right?"

"Actually," Colin objected. "Hodor's origin is unknown and I prefer to think that he was adopted by House Stark at the request of Ned's sister, Lyanna, who secretly wed a Targaryen."

"Wow," Emma said, equally impressed and worried by Colin's beyond obsessive knowledge of a show that was entirely too violent for a seven-year-old. "And Tara's cool with you watching such a graphic show?" Emma asked.

"You're saying her name wrong. It's pronounced Tar-ah, just

like Tar-garyen," Colin corrected. "And yes. Mom lets me do whatever I want."

Emma rolled her eyes. She hated spoiled kids almost as much as she hated the way everyone pronounced *Tar-ah's* name. It was like they were trying to make her sound classy and mysterious, but she would always be the home wrecking tramp from South Carolina that broke up her parents and ruined Emma's world.

"Whatever," Emma muttered, stomping past Colin and Hodor. All she wanted was to be alone, but since she didn't have a room to hide out in, she settled for plunking herself on the uncomfortable white couch. Her plan was to drown her sorrows in a mind-numbing Netflix binge. *That was if she could find the damn television remote.*

Emma searched the blank surfaces of the ridiculously modern glass furniture to no avail, and to make matters worse, Colin couldn't take a hint. He followed her around the living room so closely he was practically her shadow.

"Wanna come play in my room?" he asked. "I can teach you how to speak Dothraki."

"No. I want to watch TV."

"Cool. I like TV." Colin parked himself on the couch and Hodor curled up at his feet. "Penelope, television on."

Emma jumped when the television came to life. "How'd you do that?"

"It's a smart house," Colin replied. "You just tell Penelope what you want her to do."

If only Penelope could make annoying seven-year-olds disappear, Emma thought bitterly.

"Whatcha wanna watch?" Colin asked. "Dad gets all the channels."

Emma stilled. "What did you say?" *Did this brat actually call her father, Dad?*

"We have all the channels," Colin said loud and slow. "Just tell Penelope what you want to watch."

"What I want," Emma scathed. "Is to watch TV alone."

"Oh." Colin looked crestfallen as he slid off the couch. "I'll be in my room."

Emma almost felt bad as she watched him mope down the hall. But as he disappeared into the bedroom that should've been hers, her guilt evaporated. It wasn't her job to babysit Colin. He could call her father whatever he wanted, but that didn't make Colin her brother. *Where the hell was her father, anyway?*

Emma had been home for almost an hour and there was no sign of him or home wrecker. *Did they really leave Colin home alone?* Sure he was witty for a seven-year-old, but he was still just a kid. Her parents would've never left her alone at that age.

Two thoughts swept over Emma and both made her heart sink. Either her father and Tara had just assumed Emma would babysit Colin, or they forgot about the little boy as easily as they'd forgotten about Emma. Whatever the answer, Emma was back to feeling guilty for how she'd treated Colin. He was bratty and annoying, but none of this was his fault. And sadly, Emma wasn't sure how to make it up to him. It's not like she could be expected to know how to be a sister overnight.

She let out a groan and wrapped herself in the white blanket she'd found on the back of the couch. Cyber Penelope turned on a cheesy Christmas movie at Emma's command, and she fell into a restless sleep as she wondered how the hell her life had gotten so screwed up.

10

ill

WILL LOOKED like he'd lost a fight with his mattress when he woke up the next morning. His thick dark hair was sticking up in every direction and his gray t-shirt was disheveled. He hadn't slept well and he knew the reason why—*women*.

Between trying to get Liz to leave after dinner and spending the rest of the night messaging Emma, Will was beyond frustrated. He kept reliving their near mistletoe moment. He hadn't been able to get Emma out of his head last night. And sadly, it seemed today would be no different.

Will quickly hopped in the shower to wash away the remains of his restless night, but he knew he would be left with the look of hurt he'd seen smoldering in Emma's eyes before she stormed off last night. And the worst part was, if the elevator doors had opened five seconds later, he would've been kissing Emma, and probably had a restless night for an entirely different reason.

Scrubbing his hair vigorously, Will wished he were taking a cold shower for the usual reasons, rather than to calm the anger that was bubbling inside of him. *How could he be this stupid?* He was supposed to be over Emma by now. He'd promised himself he wouldn't go down this road again. *She'd hurt him enough.*

If anyone had the right to be pissed, it was Will. Emma was the one who stood him up at the winter formal last year. She should be the one left wanting for a change. But it seemed Emma would forever be the one shutting Will down.

He stood under the cold water for as long as he could take, but it didn't help. His mind kept wandering back to their almost kiss. He still had no idea how things had gone from perfect to poisonous in under five seconds and it was driving him insane.

Will cranked off the faucet and toweled his hair dry while throwing together an overnight bag for Cranston's, along with a shirt and tie—a prerequisite for any Cranston soiree. Next he donned jeans, a t-shirt and light blue sweater. The sweater was an early Christmas gift from his mother, just one more sign she probably wasn't coming home for the holidays. At least she'd gotten the color right—Glacier blue, the exact shade of Will's eyes.

He glanced in the mirror and winked at his reflection. He'd perfected looking like a million bucks even when his heart felt like road kill. He put on his game face, determined not to let his parents or Emma ruin his day. Maybe if he could just avoid Emma until the party tonight they would both be calm enough to have a civil discussion. Because despite how many times Will told himself he was over her, he knew it wasn't true. And it never would be until he found out what the hell happened last year.

. . .

Emma

EMMA WOKE WITH A START. Something wet coated her face as the room filled with noise. She opened her eyes, pinpointing the something wet as Hodor's slober. His panting tongue was inches from her face and Colin was standing next to him wearing Batman pajamas, cowboy boots and a ridiculous smile.

"Morning, Emma. Wanna watch cartoons with us?"

Emma rubbed her eyes groggily and looked around. "Us?"

"Me and Hodor."

"What time is it?"

Colin shrugged, but then shouted to the room. "Penelope. What time is it?"

"The time is 6:11 am, eastern standard time," the disembodied female voice replied.

Emma growled and pulled her blanket over her head.

"What cartoons do you like?" Colin asked, poking her in the shoulder.

"The kind that don't start until noon," she grumbled.

Colin laughed. "You're funny."

Emma felt him nestle next to her feet on the couch and she lost all hope that he would leave if she ignored him long enough. Colin settled on something called '*The Loud House*', which was quickly living up to its name. Emma flung off her covers, grabbed her cell phone and stomped to the bathroom.

"Might as well start my day," she mumbled to herself.

~

A hot shower and fresh clothes did help improve her mood. Emma was just adding the finishing touches to her hair and makeup while rocking out to her divas playlist on Spotify when she got a Snapchat notification. She clicked on it and her heart dropped. It was a photo of Liz and Will from last night. Liz was sitting entirely too close and feeding him pasta. The caption over the photo read: MINE.

Emma clicked on Liz's story. It was filled with photos of her and Will from last night. She knew she shouldn't look, but she couldn't stop herself and each new caption was like a punch to the gut.

DINNER WITH BOO, was the caption over the same pasta feeding pic Liz had sent directly to Emma. SNUGGLES, was typed over a pic of feet under a blanket. And the nail in the coffin was a photo of Will's lips poised for a kiss. Liz's perfectly manicured red claws were on either side of his lips and the caption read, THIS FACE IS PERFECTION.

Suddenly Emma felt ill. *How had she been so stupid?* She'd been seconds away from kissing Will yesterday. And she couldn't believe she'd spent the whole night tossing and turning over him. She'd actually felt bad about storming off after seeing Liz. Emma had let herself believe that maybe she'd overreacted and should give Will a chance to explain. But Liz's pictures did all the explaining Emma needed. Will was still the same sleaze ball he'd always been, and apparently Emma was the same sappy moron, ready to fall for him again.

11

ill

AT BREAKFAST, Sharon begged Will for what felt like the millionth time to let her order one of those plastic pre-decorated Christmas trees for the house.

"We're Taylors. We do *not* put imposter Christmas trees in this house," Will said imitating his father's booming voice.

"William, can you please be serious?"

"I *am* serious, Sharon. This is probably my last Christmas at home. And I'm not going to be the first Taylor in history to break our holiday tradition."

"I'm not suggesting you break tradition, hun. If your parents get home in time you can still go chop down your perfect Christmas tree and drag it back here."

Will waved her off. "Then we'd have two trees."

"So, what's wrong with that? Lord knows this house is big enough for a dozen trees."

"We don't need two trees. One perfect tree from Emmerich Tree Farm is just fine."

"I just don't want you to be disappointed," Sharon argued, topping off Will's coffee.

"I won't. They'll be here, Sharon. I know my parents have been MIA lately, but they wouldn't miss Christmas."

Sharon shook her head at his stubbornness and muttered something under her breath. "I'm going to the market today. Any special requests?"

"No thanks. And I won't be home for dinner tonight, so don't worry about making me anything."

"And where will you be going?" Sharon asked, in a more motherly tone than Will's actual mother ever managed.

"Cranston's."

"Parker Cranston?"

Will nodded.

Sharon clucked her tongue with disapproval. "That boy is trouble. Don't let him drag you into any."

"Yes, Mom," Will mocked, giving Sharon a quick peck on the cheek as he grabbed an apple and retreated from the kitchen before she could continue her rant.

It's not that Sharon didn't have a point. Parker Cranston's reputation as Manhattan's millionaire party boy wasn't without merit. But he and Will had been friends since their overpriced preschool days.

It was true that Cranston had gotten Will into his fair share of trouble over the years, but he always got him out. That was one of the many benefits of being Cranston's friend. Another was his lavish parties. And Will was sure tonight would be no exception.

Will shrugged on a coat and shined the crisp green apple on his blue sweater as he walked down the hallway toward the elevator. He knew the party wouldn't be starting for hours, but he figured he'd head over to Cranston's anyway. There was always a group of his buddies hanging around the hotel suite pre-gaming and playing video games. Neither were really Will's preferred hobbies, but it beat sitting around his house alone all day.

He'd just taken a big bite out of his apple when Emma emerged into the hallway like an apparition. She was dressed in winter white from head to toe and her blonde hair cascaded down her back. She looked so beautiful Will stopped short. He must've forgotten how to chew too because he started to choke on his bite of apple.

Emma turned, seeming startled to find Will staring at her. When her surprise passed, it was replaced with an angry glare.

"Stalk much?" she muttered.

"I'm not stalking you."

"Oh really? What do they call hiding out in the hallway these days?"

"I'm not hiding."

Emma rolled her eyes. "Whatever."

"Good morning to you, too," Will snapped.

"Is it a good morning, Will?"

"It was."

"Well good for you," Emma snarled, making her way to the elevator without waiting for Will.

He tried to shake off her rudeness. Emma had never been a morning person, but this was ridiculous. *Just get her to the party,* he reminded himself.

"So," Will began, hoping to start over. "What are you up to today?"

"None of your business."

"Shit, Emma. Are you ever gonna tell me what I did to piss you off? Or are you just gonna hold it against me forever?"

"Are you serious?"

"Yes!"

The elevator dinged and the doors yawned wide, stretching

out the tension between them. Emma was the first to move. She blew out a breath of frustration and marched onto the elevator.

Will followed closely behind her. "Well? Do I get an explanation?"

Emma huffed. "Why don't you ask Liz?"

"Because I'm asking you."

Emma crossed her arms stubbornly. It was Will's turn to sigh. Emma had a stubborn stream as long as the Hudson River. If she didn't want to tell him why she was pissed he knew he should just drop it. *Even if everything inside him was screaming not to.*

Will decided to change tactics. If he could make Emma laugh maybe it would help break the iceberg forming between them. He glanced up at the mistletoe that seemed to be mocking him. He nudged Emma lightly with his elbow and nodded to the presumptuous plant. "We keep finding ourselves here."

"So?"

"Maybe it's a sign."

"If you think I'm going to kiss you, you're an even bigger idiot than I gave you credit for."

"I'd settle for an awkward high-five," Will suggested, raising one hand in the air.

Emma left him hanging. The elevator doors dinged open again, and before Will could say anything else, a little old lady decked out in a fur coat that matched her tiny dog got on. They all rode the elevator in silence to the lobby. Will practically had to chase Emma down once she exited the lift. He caught up to her on the street where she was hailing a cab.

"So I'll see you tonight?" Will asked trying to mask the hope in his voice.

"Tonight?"

"Cranston's party."

"I'm not going to that."

"I thought we were going together?"

Emma laughed, but there was no joy in it. "I'm not going to that party with you. I'm not going anywhere with you."

Will's patience finally snapped. "Why?" he shouted.

He was done playing this game. It had gone on long enough and it was getting him nowhere. If Emma was ready to throw him away he was damn sure not going down without a fight. "What the hell did I do, Emma?"

"It doesn't matter."

Will raked his hands through his damp hair in frustration. "Obviously it does."

"Maybe it did, but not anymore."

A cab pulled up and Emma started to pull the door open, but Will slammed it shut. "Emma, can you just talk to me?"

"About what?"

"How about why you're so eager to throw us away?"

"There *is* no *us*, Will."

"Really? Ten years of friendship means nothing to you? We were best friends, Emma. And you just left like it was nothing."

Tears were pooling in Emma's green eyes and Will reached up to brush them away but she pushed him back.

"Don't," she snapped.

"Just tell me why, Emma."

"Get it through your head, Will. I don't want anything to do with you."

"Then what do you want?"

"I want this stupid holiday to be over so I can go back to forgetting about you." She yanked open the cab door. "And if you really want to know why it's so easy for me to walk away, why don't you ask Liz?" Then Emma got in the cab, slammed the door and was gone.

Will watched the yellow cab until it disappeared into the busy Manhattan traffic. He felt like his heart had been slammed in the cab door and run over by every car that sped past. He gulped down cold breaths of air trying to regain his composure. He was grateful he hadn't eaten a big breakfast, because his stomach was tying itself in knots. Will wasn't used to fighting with people, especially not his friends. And having pissed off a friend for an unknown reason was it's own particular brand of torture. But Will planned on ending this feud tonight. If Liz knew why Emma was so determined to think the worst of him then he was damn sure going to confront her about it at Cranston's party.

12

Emma

EMMA HADN'T KNOWN where she was going when she left her apartment, only that she needed to get out of her father's cold white prison. Her fight with Will hadn't helped her mood at all. She sobbed in the back seat of the yellow cab, feeling even more adrift than ever.

The cab driver didn't appreciate her indecisiveness and after changing her mind three times about her destination, he rudely told her to get out in Brooklyn. Emma wandered from cafés to boutiques missing the days of having her own driver. Her feet were cold and wet. Louboutin boots were fashionable as hell, but definitely not designed to trudge through the slushy winter sidewalks of Brooklyn.

She eventually took a cab back to Midtown and spent the rest of the day wandering the garment district, stopping at her favorite fashion houses. But shopping without her old

Manhattan budget wasn't much fun. Even if Emma had managed to swipe her father's black card, she had a feeling it wouldn't fix the hollow ache in her chest. So she went to church. The church of fashion that is—Mood Fabrics.

Mood was a fashion designer's heaven on earth. A maze of rainbows and glitter, with rows upon rows of luxurious fabric bolts stacked to the ceiling, and an accessory section that sparkled brighter than the Crown Jewels. Emma used to spend hours lost among the aisles dreaming of the day she'd be in design school at Parsons and shopping here for real. She always left feeling inspired. But today, even Mood couldn't make her smile.

She knew if she still felt dismal after spending the day in New York's fashion mecca that it was a lost cause. Out of options, Emma hailed a cab and headed home—*if that's even what she could call her father's new ice palace.*

Emma checked her phone from the back seat of the cab. The screen was blowing up with notifications. Apparently word that she was back in town had spread through the St. James social-sphere. Everyone was asking if she was coming to Cranston's party tonight. Even before her run in with Will this morning, she'd decided she wasn't going. The pictures of Will and Liz still seared her heart. And Emma had no intention of witnessing their affection first hand.

She swiped to another screen on her phone. She had two missed calls from her mother. Emma sighed and decided to call her back. Her mother answered on the first ring.

"Hey, sweetheart. How are you?"

"Hi, Mom. I'm fine."

"Really? You don't sound fine. Are things going well with your father?"

Emma's throat felt tight with tears. Things were definitely not going well, but Emma couldn't tell her mother that. *How could she tell her that her father was marrying Tara, the woman that ruined their marriage, because she's pregnant? Or that his new apartment only has one extra bedroom, which belongs to the home wrecker's son, because Emma's own father forgot she was coming for Christmas? But more than anything, how could Emma tell her mother she just wanted to come back to Boston, because New York wasn't home anymore?*

"Everything's fine, Mom. It's just weird being back in New York."

"Are you going to get to see any of your old friends?" her mother asked.

"Probably not."

"What about Kensie?"

"No. Her family's still in France."

"Oh I'm sorry, sweetheart. I know you miss her. What about Will? You guys used to be so close. Do you have any plans to meet up with him?"

Emma swallowed hard. "I already did."

"Oh that's great, sweetie. How is he?"

"The same."

"Emma, are you sure everything's okay?"

"Everything's fine, Mom."

"So tell me, what else is new?"

"Nothing much," Emma replied.

"Oh come on, Emma. You've gotta tell me something. What's your father's new apartment like?"

"White."

"White?"

Emma could practically here her mother's eyebrows

arching in surprise and it made her smile and miss her even more. "Yeah. As in everything is white."

Her mother giggled. "Well that's something."

"And he got a dog."

Her mother gasped and Emma loved her for it. "No! He said he'd never get a dog."

"He said he'd never do a lot of things," Emma grumbled. "Like leave us."

"Emma, sweetheart. You know your father didn't leave you. The problems in our marriage were between us. And no matter what happens, your father still loves you very much. I know the divorce put you in the middle, and I'm sorry for that, sweetheart."

"I love you, Mom."

"Oh, baby, I love you too. So much. Are you sure you're all right?"

"Yeah. I think it's just different than I was expecting."

"Emma, I know this is a big change, but give it a chance."

"I will."

"And you know you can come home anytime you want, right? No one is forcing you to spend Christmas with your father. The last thing I want is for this to be any harder on you than it is already."

"Thanks, Mom. I love you."

"I love you too."

13

ill

THE SUN WAS STARTING to set by the time Cranston decided to grace his hotel suite with his presence. He waltzed in in true Parker Cranston style, with a bottle of obscenely expensive booze and a girl on each arm.

He greeted Will and the half dozen other guys from St. James that had already gathered at his place with a wry smile. “Gentleman, let the festivities begin.”

“I’m afraid we started without ya,” Vaughn Bettencourt replied, holding up a bong.

“Well, then I’d better catch up.” Cranston turned to the women accompanying him. “Ladies, go ahead and get started.”

“Are they the models?” Mason Spaulding asked, taking his eyes off the video game he was playing.

“Chill, Mason.” Cranston smirked. “The models are arriving with the martinis.”

"I thought the theme was mistletoe and martinis?" Will asked.

Cranston grinned. "I thought it was missing that something special."

"Yeah, models!" Mason said, high-fiving Vaughn.

"Martinis, mistletoe and models," Will mused. "It has a nice ring to it."

Cranston winked. "My sentiments exactly."

Will laughed and drained the last of his scotch, before pouring himself another. It had lightened his mood substantially.

Cranston poured himself a drink and joined Will on the couch. "What's the occasion?" he asked nodding to Will's glass.

Will rarely drank, and when he did, it was usually beer. He found himself surprised that Cranston knew him so well. But Will was going to need more than a few glasses of scotch before he'd ever admit he was nursing a broken heart in front of Cranston and half the guys on his lacrosse team.

"*Emma's not coming*," Mason added in a mocking tone.

Will chucked a pillow at Mason's head. "Shut up."

Cranston raised an eyebrow. "Emma who?"

Will sighed. "Emma Rhodes."

"She's back?"

Will nodded. "For Christmas break."

"And let me guess, she was so much fun at the winter formal last year you asked her for a repeat performance?" Cranston teased.

Will shook his head. "Ya know, you guys are kinda the worst?"

"Accurate," Cranston crooned. "But relax, I'll let you have first dibs on the models."

"Models aren't going to fix this problem," Will replied.

Cranston smirked. "I haven't found too many problems models can't fix. Well . . . models and money."

The guys laughed and ribbed Will a bit more. Luckily one of the hotel staff pulled Cranston away with a question, and everyone else went back to their video game. Will snuck away to the balcony, letting the cold New York air bite his skin. He glanced at his phone, his finger hovering above Emma's name. He wanted to text her, but the idea of going round two wasn't appealing. Instead, he scrolled down his contacts to another name and tapped out a message.

Will: Hey. Are you coming tonight?
Liz: That depends. Will you be there?
Will: I'm already here.
Liz: Then I'm as good as there.
Will: Good. We need to talk.
Liz: Looking forward to it.

14

Emma

EMMA FELT WORSE after talking to her mother. She hated keeping things from her. They'd always been so close. And before the divorce, they told each other everything. But the scandal of her father's affair had changed things. It happened right around the same time that Will broke Emma's heart. Emma had wanted to talk to her mother about it, but she was either crying or raging over her father's betrayal. There just never seemed like a good time for Emma to tell her mother about her own boy trouble.

She tried to deal with her complicated feelings for Will on her own, but managed to royally screw things up. Not only had she lost the possibility of dating him, but she'd also lost his friendship. And Emma didn't know what hurt worse.

That had been the worst year of her life. And even though Boston wasn't where she wanted to be, Emma thought she was putting her life back together. Her mother had a great job, they'd settled into their new home and Emma was looking forward to applying to fashion schools. In a few short months, her life would start again. This trip to Manhattan was meant to help her make her decision between pursuing her college aspirations in New York or Boston. And so far, New York had shown her the cold shoulder.

Emma had never felt like such an outsider before. She'd been so excited to return home and spend the holiday with her father. She'd done her best to put a positive spin on her parents' divorce lately. Telling herself she'd get to be one of those kids who got two of everything. Two birthdays, two Christmases, two graduation parties. And it would great, because she'd get the undivided attention of her father at each—something she never had before because he worked too much.

She'd been sure this trip home would be the start of something great—that her father would want to spend time with her now that he got to see her so rarely. *God, she was stupid.* Her father might have divorced her mother, but Emma certainly felt like she'd been cut out of his life just the same.

The chime of a text message interrupted Emma's pity party. She looked at her phone to see a message from Marcy Foy lighting up her screen. *Why was Marcy texting her?* They weren't even friends when they were classmates. And according to Will, Marcy was only concerned about beating out Liz for ruling monarch at St. James. *Did she really think Emma was going to help her?*

Marcy: Hey bitch, heard you're back in town. Going to Cranston's tonight?
Emma: I'm just here for xmas. I'm not going to Cranston's.
Marcy: You have to come. Who else is gonna get drunk and make fun of Liz Slander-smear with me?

Emma laughed. The offer was enticing. An old quote floated back to her mind. *'The enemy of my enemy is my friend.'* Emma couldn't remember where it came from, but she finally felt like she understood it. Having someone loathe Liz as much as Emma did was suddenly comforting.

Emma: Enticing. But I'm spending time with family.
Marcy: Oh come on. We can use my father's app to give her a bad nose job.

Marcy's father was *the* plastic surgeon in Manhattan. Everyone on the Upper East Side went to him. It was rumored that he let Marcy have a nose job in fifth grade, and then boobs in eighth. He also developed an app called Snip that let you try out different plastic surgery options. Of course Marcy and her friends used it to edit photos and give their fr-enemies big noses or double chins.

Emma: Sorry. Maybe next time.
Marcy: Well, if you change your mind, you know where I'll be. Enjoy family time.

Family time. What a joke. Tara and Colin were *not* family. All Emma wanted was to spend time with her father, but she'd only seen him for a total of twenty minutes in the two days she'd been in New York. Her mother's words echoed in Emma's mind. *No matter what happens, your father still loves you very much.* Maybe Emma could ask to spend some time together, just the two of them. *That is if she ever got two seconds alone with him.*

Emma was feeling sorry for herself when she walked into her father's apartment. And it didn't help that she nearly ran into Tara in the foyer. She looked impeccable in a new designer dress that Emma had coveted while window-shopping. The jade fabric hugged Tara in all the right places, highlighting the slightest hint of a baby bump.

"Emma, honey. I'm so glad I caught you," Tara chirped. "I'm on my way out to meet your father. Colin's in his room. Would you mind ordering some dinner for him a little later? And order yourself anything you'd like as well."

Tara slipped two crisp hundred-dollar bills from her red Gucci clutch and tried handing them to Emma, but she took a step back.

"No. I'm not your babysitter, Tara. And since I know you're only marrying my father for his money, why don't you use some of it to hire some help."

Tara's eyes were wide and she seemed to struggle to find words as she gawked at Emma.

"Forget it," Emma grumbled, turning on her heels and exiting the apartment while Tara's shocked face stared after her.

Emma stormed down the hall. She hadn't planned to go to Cranston's stupid party, but right now it was the best offer she had. She pulled out her phone and typed out a quick message.

Emma: You were right. I need a drink. See you at Cranston's.
Marcy: I'm always right.

15

ill

Liz was late as usual. And when she arrived, Will wasted no time cornering her.

"Hey, we need to talk."

"Hey, handsome. I'm happy to see you, too," she crooned, trying to plant a kiss on his lips.

Will turned his face and gave her his cheek instead. Liz was with her usual crew of drama queens, Isabelle Spence and Paris Dillon. The last thing Will needed was those gossip girls blowing his conversation with Liz out of proportion and posting it all over social media. Last year they'd slut shamed a freshman girl for sleeping with Cranston to the point that she dropped out of St. James. It was total crap. Sleeping with Cranston was practically a badge of honor for girls at St. James. But apparently Paris had a thing for him so the poor freshman got the hazing of her life when they posted a video of her and Cranston getting it on.

That type of bullshit was the precise reason Will didn't have any form of social media. He knew it didn't stop the drama from happening, but it could at least keep him from getting dragged into it by not giving himself the option to participate.

Will grabbed Liz's hand and started leading her away from her friends and their prying ears.

"Where are we going?" she asked, her voice flirty as ever.

"To talk."

"Where?"

"Anywhere but here."

"Aren't you the man of mystery?"

Will could hear Isabelle and Paris giggling in the hall as he pulled Liz into one of the hotel suite's many bedrooms and shut the door. But when he turned to face Liz, he knew instantly it'd been a mistake to bring her into a bedroom.

Emma

WALKING into Cranston's party made Emma feel like she'd never left New York. It seemed some things had stayed the same. Like the fact that Parker Cranston threw the best illicit parties in Manhattan. The festivities were in full swing and Cranston had outdone himself. The penthouse suite of his father's swanky hotel had been transformed into a glittering wonderland of red and green, complete with DJ, strobe lights, mirrored dance floor and more mistletoe than Emma had ever seen before. The entire ceiling was draped with it.

Emma handed her coat and purse to the coat check girl, who was dressed as a very naughty elf, then scanned the party for Marcy. It was impossible to pick anyone out of the crowd.

The only people that stuck out were the scantily clad cocktail waitresses wearing Santa hats and not much else. As Emma watched them carrying trays of decadent-looking martinis through the throngs of party goers, a shiver of déjà vu swept through her. Suddenly, it was junior year all over again and she was staring into a sea of familiar St. James faces, but only searching for one—*Will.*

Coming here had been a mistake. Emma retreated to the coat check and handed her ticket over. If she could retrieve her things quickly, she could disappear before anyone noticed her. Emma tapped her heel impatiently, while the naughty elf went in search of her things. *What the hell was taking her so long?*

Finally the girl returned and Emma thanked her, draping her purse and jacket over her arm in a hurry. She breathed a sigh of relief that no one had spotted her and spun on her heel ready to flee from the party. But then disaster struck—in the form of Parker Cranston. Emma slammed into his chest and nearly fell on her ass as a result. Cranston grinned at her, not even offering a hand to steady her. She dropped her purse, but managed to stay upright. He spoke as she bent to pick it up.

"Emma Rhodes. So nice of you to grace us with your presence," Cranston drawled in his usual smarmy manner.

"Hey, Cranston."

"You weren't going to leave without saying hello, were you?" he asked, nodding to her jacket. "Although I hear that's your MO."

"No, I-I was just cold," Emma stuttered.

Cranston raised a well-manicured finger lazily into the air and a cocktail waitress appeared at his side. He pulled two bright red martinis off the tray and handed one to Emma. "This will keep the chill away."

"Oh, um, thanks."

Cranston draped his free hand around the waitress's slim hips and began leading her away. But he paused and called back to Emma over his shoulder. "Be sure to say hello to your boyfriend before you disappear again. He really hates it when you leave without saying goodbye."

Guilt bloomed in Emma's stomach. "Will isn't my boyfriend," she called, but Cranston was already disappearing into the crowd. "He never was," she whispered, letting the painful truth of her words sink in.

Yes, coming here had definitely been a mistake. Emma drained her martini and shrugged on her coat as the alcohol spread through her like liquid fire. It was cinnamon flavored and warmed her chest from the inside out, but did little to dull her despair. As she walked toward the elevator, Emma realized it would take a lot more than a few martinis to erase the sting of this awful holiday from her heart.

Just as the doors rolled open, Emma heard a shrill voice call her name.

"Emma Rhodes! You better not be ditching me!"

Emma turned to see Marcy Foy grinning at her. Her auburn hair was perfectly styled and her skintight black dress spoke volumes of her father's flawless surgery skills. Marcy teetered closer in her towering stilettos and wrapped Emma in a tipsy hug before passing her one of the booze syringes she was clutching in her pale hands. They were Cranston's specialty, and guaranteed to get you good and drunk.

"Drink up," Marcy ordered. "You've got some catching up to do."

Emma tried to protest, but Marcy was already downing her shot. She gave a full body shiver when she was done and howled. "Damn these are amazing. I really need to trick Cranston into giving me his secret recipe."

Emma still clutched her plastic syringe of alcohol, staring longingly at the elevator doors as they closed without her inside.

Marcy was uncapping another shot when she noticed Emma wasn't drinking hers. "Emma, drink up bitch."

Emma exhaled, remembering why she'd never really gotten along with Marcy. The girl was bossy as hell, and when she was drunk it only magnified things.

"Actually, I think I'm gonna call it a night," Emma replied.

"What? You just got here! And we haven't even played Snip!"

"I don't think I'm in the mood anymore."

"Oh come on. Have one drink with me, Emma."

Saying no was never Emma's strong suit. She wavered as Marcy tugged on her hand with a pleading smile. Emma didn't feel like partying with her old friends, *or frienemies*, for that matter. Especially if they were going to treat her like Cranston had. But the idea of going back to her father's to babysit Colin wasn't any more appealing.

"Em, you're already here. And I'm guessing it's because hanging out with your father's new family is as awful as it sounds."

Emma cringed. "Did everybody know he's marrying Tara but me?"

Marcy's eyes widened. "Oh shit! You didn't know?"

Emma shook her head. "Nope, my father saved that bombshell for my Christmas visit."

"Damn. That's cold."

"And it gets better. Tara's pregnant."

"No!" Marcy held her shot out to Emma. "You need this way more than I do."

Emma laughed, realizing how ridiculous her life must sound. She took the shot from Marcy and swallowed it in one gulp. It tasted like peppermint and burned her throat on the way down, but to Emma's surprise, it did the trick. The sharp edges of her self-pity began to blur. She took another shot and giggled. "Thanks. That helps, actually."

Marcy looked at her with understanding. "So your father's an ass. Mine is too. But that doesn't mean they get to ruin our night. Come on, let's get drunk and dance."

Emma shook her head. "I don't think shots and dancing is going to solve my problems."

Marcy grinned. "Maybe not, but it certainly beats worrying about things you can't change. Plus, martinis make everything better."

Emma shrugged, realizing Marcy was right. *Why shouldn't she be young and reckless? It's what her father was doing.*

Emma stopped resisting and let Marcy drag her back toward the party. For a tiny girl, Marcy was deceptively strong. Maybe it was martini muscles, but Emma couldn't break Marcy's grasp. And before she knew it, Marcy had tossed Emma's things back at the naughty elf's coat check and dragged her onto the dance floor.

16

ill

WILL BACKED AWAY FROM LIZ. She had a seductive look on her face that he didn't like. His retreat didn't stop her. It only made her move closer. She slipped her slender arms around his neck.

"You smell nice," she murmured against him.

"Liz . . . "

"Hmm?"

Will unhooked her arms and took a step back.

Liz only smiled further and started to slip the lace straps of her black dress from her shoulders.

Will reached out to stop her. "Liz. I want to talk. Just talk."

Disappointment flickered across her pretty face. "Really?"

Will sighed, not knowing where to start. He had to be careful when it came to Liz. She's been part of his life forever and it was something that would never change. His parents were best friends with hers. The family names Vanderveer and

Taylor were practically synonymous with one another. Their businesses were beyond intertwined, sponsoring everything from joint charities to international ventures. And it seemed their children were no exception.

Liz's older sister, Hazel, was married to Will's second eldest brother, Tom. And ever since that merger, it seemed everyone in the Vanderveer and Taylor families had decided Will and Liz would be the next acquisition. And that plan seemed to be music to Liz's ears.

Ever since Hazel got engaged to Tom, Liz practically branded Will as hers, chasing away any other girl who tried to get close. And it wasn't entirely Liz's fault. Their mothers were always saying things like, *'look how cute they are together'*, or, *'how perfect would it be if they got married?'* It was no wonder Liz had gotten the wrong idea about Will. But he didn't know what to do. He'd only ever had eyes for one girl—Emma.

Over the years, Will had tried to be a gentleman and stave off Liz's advances delicately. But it seemed no matter how many times he told her they were just friends, Liz chose to ignore him. And that was the hard part. They *were* friends. *At least Will thought they were.*

Sometimes Liz could be really cool. Like the night Emma stood him up at the formal and Liz came out in the freezing cold to drag him inside. Even though she was there with a date, she'd saved him a dance. And when Will tried to say he just wanted to go home Liz had said, "You deserve at least one good memory from tonight," and dragged him onto the dance floor.

That had turned the night around for him. Will had been prepared to spend his junior formal drinking peppermint schnapps from Cranston's flask and sulking at their table. But Liz refused to let him. The night hadn't gone as planned, but Liz had helped it not be a total disaster. She'd even been there for him in the weeks that followed, when Emma stopped coming to school.

Will knew Liz wasn't walking him to class or sitting with him at lunch for completely selfless reasons. And letting her do it was definitely leading her on. But the truth was, Will had needed her. He felt lost when Emma left, and having Liz around distracted him from the pain for a bit. Will often felt guilty about letting Liz in when he knew in his heart he still had feelings for Emma. But then he would think about how Emma had just left, completely cutting him off like he was nothing. And then he felt nothing but anger. *Why should he feel guilty?* He hadn't done anything wrong. Except maybe ask Emma out in the first place.

No. Asking her out wasn't a mistake. It wouldn't still hurt like this if it were.

Will had known there was something special about Emma since they were ten years old. He realized now that he'd probably loved her even then, even before he knew what love was. But Will had been an idiot, too scared to make a move and when he finally did he'd messed it up somehow. But he wasn't going to make that mistake again. This was his chance to find out what went wrong that night and fix it.

"Will? Is everything okay? You're sorta freaking me out with all the broody pacing."

Will looked up. He hadn't realized he was pacing. "Sorry. Everything's fine. Or at least, I think it will be. But I need your help with something."

"What?"

"Emma."

"Emma?" Liz's whole demeanor changed. She crossed her arms and her red lips twisted into a tense scowl. "Why the hell would I help that Park Ave pretender?"

"Because it would be helping me."

Liz rolled her eyes.

"I'm serious, Liz. Emma and I keep getting in the same fight about last year's formal. She won't tell me why she stood me up or moved without saying goodbye."

"Will, that was last year. I don't know what her problem is but she should get over it."

"Well she's not. And neither am I."

"So what does any of this have to do with me?" Liz asked.

"Emma won't tell me why she's pissed at me but she seems to think you know why."

Liz stared down at her perfect red nails as if examining them for flaws. "I don't know why'd she'd say that."

But she did. Will knew it. He'd known Liz his entire life. And he knew when she was lying because she could never look him in the eye. "Liz, I think you do."

"This is bullshit, Will. And I'm not going to stand here and let you accuse me like this when I've been nothing but good to you."

Liz stalked toward the door and Will reached for her hand. "Liz—"

"No!" she yelled, shaking his grasp. Liz took a deep breath, blowing it out dramatically. "I don't know if you're drunk or what, but you're lucky it's almost Christmas and I'm in a forgiving mood. I'm willing to pretend this never happened. But this discussion is over."

And with that, Liz sashayed out the door, leaving Will more confused than ever.

Emma

MARCY WAS RIGHT, dancing did solve problems. *Well, dancing and copious amounts of alcohol.* Emma lost track of the number of shots and martinis she'd had. All she knew was shaking it on the dance floor was making her feel better than she had in a long time. She and Marcy twirled and giggled until the whole world seemed to melt into one big blur of light, taking the stress of the past few days with it.

Emma had a sudden urge to update her blog post. She had her holiday survival guide all wrong. She smirked to herself as she mentally revised it.

A Haute Chic's Holiday Survival Guide

1. *Family drama is much easier to swallow with a martini.*
2. *Avoid cute heartbreaking neighbors at all costs.*
3. *Under no circumstances get caught under the mistletoe.*
4. *When all else fails, dance.*

Emma continued tearing up the dance floor with Marcy. At some point, they'd been joined by Isabelle Spence and Paris Dillon. At first Emma had been surprised to see the superficial girls unattached from Liz Vanderveer's ass. But after a few more drinks, Emma forgot to care and let the music carry her away.

She was thoroughly busting a move when a Santa-clad cocktail waitress roved by with a fresh tray of martinis. Emma was tipsy on her heels, but narrowly managed to move out of the waitress's way, avoiding a near disaster. But two seconds later Emma heard a shriek, followed by a tidal wave of cold red liquid. Sticky alcohol dripped from Emma as she turned to see the mortified waitress kneeling next to her overturned tray of drinks. The crowd booed and laughed as the waitress tried to pick of the pieces of shattered glass. She locked eyes with Emma, apologizing for dumping red martinis all over her white dress, but Emma barely heard her. She was staring at Liz Vanderveer, who was watching the dance floor disaster with the smug satisfaction of someone who'd gotten exactly what she wanted.

"I'm so sorry," the waitress babbled at Emma. "I swear, someone pushed me. I never trip."

"It's okay," Emma replied, taking the napkins the girl offered to wipe off her dripping arms. "I believe you."

"Oh my God, your dress is ruined. I'll pay for it, I swear. Please don't say anything to Mr. Cranston. I really need this job."

"I won't. And it's not a big deal. Look, everyone's forgotten about it already."

And they had. The dance floor was pulsing with bodies again. Most of them were obliviously dancing over the broken martini glasses and it wasn't as if the floor wasn't already tacky with spilled drinks. Yes, everyone had moved on, except for Liz, who was glaring at Emma with predatory hunger. Isabelle and Paris ran to her side like dogs with their tails between their legs. And Liz beckoned Emma with a finger.

Rather than publicly endure whatever else Liz had in store for her, Emma decided to follow her off the dance floor. To her surprise, Marcy came with her. She was probably there more for the gossip than moral support, but Emma still felt slightly better that she wasn't facing off with the ice queen on her own.

They assembled near the rear balcony—Liz, and her henchmaids, Isabelle and Paris. And Emma with a tipsy Marcy in tow. The cold air rushed in from the balcony doors making Emma shiver. They were far enough from the DJ to talk now, but Liz looked like she'd rather throw Emma over the balcony than have a conversation.

Liz looked Emma up and down with disgust, "Listen, Emmy, I can tell from the dress you're wearing that you're clinging to last year's fashion, but I want to make something very clear for you. It's not last year. Will is with me now. It's time you get over it."

Emma's brain was fuzzy as she struggled for a come back. "I *am* over him."

"That's not what he just told me," Liz replied. "He said you won't leave him alone and you keep bringing up last year's formal. I mean really, Emma, I know you're desperate, but that's cruel, even for you. Don't you think you hurt him enough?"

"I wasn't trying to hurt him," Emma argued. "But—"

Liz took a step toward her, cutting her off. "Well you did. I should know. I was there to pick up the pieces. And maybe you find pleasure in toying with guys, but Will is mine. And I protect what's mine, Emma. So why don't you do what you do best and leave."

All the grief Emma had worked so hard to keep at bay with alcohol and dancing came crashing back, topped with a new guilt for how she'd treated Will. Liz was the second person tonight who told Emma that she'd hurt him by not showing up for the formal. *But what had he expected? Did Will really think Emma would go to the dance with him two days after he'd had sex with Liz Vanderveer? Or did he just think he'd never get caught?*

Emma was glad she'd seen the photos of Liz and Will together or she never would have believed it. They'd been at a party at Cranston's and ended up in a closet together on a some dare. Someone had opened the closet and snapped a couple photos of them in a compromising position and Paris had shared them on Snapchat.

Emma had actually been on her way to Cranston's party when she got the blast. It hit her like a dagger to the heart. Will had just asked Emma to the winter formal two days prior, so she'd spent nearly an hour getting ready for Cranston's party, convincing herself that it was finally time that she tell Will how she felt. She'd foolishly thought Cranston's party would be the start of something great for her and Will. Instead, it had been the end.

The photos from that night flew around the St. James

gossip-sphere like wildfire. And even though the images of Will and Liz's tangled limbs had been burned into Emma's memory, she still prayed for it to somehow be a bad joke. But when Emma showed up at school the next day and saw them standing together, Liz's arm, looped through Will's, something twisted in Emma's heart and she knew it was true.

Finding out Will wasn't the guy she'd always thought he was had hurt more than Emma had been willing to admit. But she refused to let herself be made a fool of. Emma knew first hand what betrayal did to a relationship and she was determined not to end up like her parents—*no matter how much she loved Will.*

And now, standing on Cranston's balcony a year later, being berated by Liz and her friends, Emma remembered precisely why she'd chosen to move to Boston with her mother and leave all this drama and heartache behind.

Emma wished she could think of something stinging or witty to say to Liz to pay the vindictive girl back for all the pain she'd caused, but Emma had never been particularly sharp-tongued, and the alcohol wasn't helping her in that department. Truthfully, the euphoric feeling the drinks had given her earlier was rapidly fading. The martinis were turning against her and Emma suddenly felt sick. The last thing she needed was to puke in the middle of the party and give Liz more ammunition to use against her, so she muttered goodbye to Marcy and headed back through the crowd to leave.

17

ill

WILL FINALLY GATHERED himself enough to leave the bedroom. He'd been ready to storm after Liz and shake the truth out of her, but he knew that wasn't the answer. He'd stayed in the room until he was sure he had his temper in check. But once outside, the pulsing lights and blaring music put him on edge again. This was the last place Will felt like being tonight. He hadn't even wanted to come once he found out Emma wasn't coming. *What the hell was he thinking telling Cranston to throw a party to win Emma back?* He couldn't even hear himself think in here, let alone try to talk through a year of misunderstanding.

He'd made up his mind to take off when a flash of white caught Will's eye. It was Emma, her white dress cutting a path through the packed dance floor toward the exit. Will was moving in an instant.

. . .

Emma

Emma was halfway through the dance floor when she slipped. She went down hard, feeling a sharp pain in her knees as they made impact with the sticky floor. *Could this night get any worse?*

Before she could answer that question, two hands reached down from the darkness to pull her to her feet. She steadied herself to thank the kind stranger, but of course it wasn't a stranger at all. Will stood before her, looking as white knight as ever. He wore a white dress shirt, untucked and a thin gray tie. His dark hair was rumpled and his smile was heart-stopping.

"Are you okay?" he asked.

"I'm great," she said as the room swayed. Emma felt herself sway with it until Will caught her again.

"You don't look great. I think you should sit down," he said leading her from the dance floor to the nearest chairs.

Will nabbed two bottles of water on their way as Emma limped behind him. He caught the hitch in her step and a look of concern passed over his face. "Are you hurt?"

"I don't think so," she mumbled and Will helped her into a ridiculously modern chair that looked more like the letter S than a piece of furniture.

"Why are you limping?" Will asked.

"Hmm?" She'd already forgotten the question. It was hard to focus with the flashing lights and swaying room. She squinted at Will. *Were there two of him?* He pulled an identical S chair close and sat down in front of her. "Em, are you okay?"

Emma giggled, watching Will try to settle all six-foot-three of him into the odd chair.

"What's so funny?" Will asked.

"You look silly."

"Me? What about you? What happened to your dress?"

Emma shrugged. "Martinis."

Will raised his eyebrows. "How many have you had?"

"A few."

"As in a few too many?" Will asked.

"Maybe," Emma slurred.

"How 'bout you let me take you home?"

"I don't think Liz would like that."

"I don't care what Liz likes," Will replied. "I care about you, Em."

Emma's heart jumped, but she pulled away from Will when he reached for her hand. Emma realized that they were sitting rather close together and she straightened up, crossing her legs as a barrier. The action sent a stab of pain through her knee and she winced.

"Shit, Emma! You're bleeding!"

"What?"

"Your leg," Will said jumping into action. He left the chair behind and knelt next to her, gently touching her left leg just below her knee. "I think there's a piece of glass in it."

"What!" Emma looked down and sure enough something other than blood shimmered from the slice in her skin. "Omigod, get it out! Get it out!"

"Hold on."

Liz! Emma was going to kill her. None of this would be happening if she hadn't pushed that cocktail waitress into Emma on the dance floor. No one had cleaned up the glass and now Emma was paying for it. She let a tiny sob escape. *Why had she ever thought martinis were the answer?*

Will slipped her shoe off and poured some of his water bottle over the wound. Emma watched a stream of blood wash down her leg and a heat wave of nausea crashed over her. She started shaking. Emma hated blood. Ever since she was a little kid even the smallest drop of it would make her queasy.

"Em, take a deep breath, you're gonna be fine. It's only a tiny cut."

Emma squeezed her eyes shut, fighting the urge to pass out.

She felt Will clasp her hand. "Em, you with me?"

Emma swayed as her vision began to tunnel. "I hate blood," she squeaked.

"I remember."

"Make it stop," she whispered. "Please make it stop, Will."

Will

THE PLEADING TONE of Emma's voice broke Will's heart. This was much worse than a crying girl. This was Emma crying. *His Emma.* And listening to her begging him to make the pain stop was enough to make him want to lasso the moon. He knew she hated blood. He couldn't believe she hadn't already passed out at the sight of it.

Once, she'd gotten a bloody nose on the playground while on the swings. She passed out, fell off and broke her arm. Will had never been more scared than he was when he watched the ambulance take Emma away. He was devastated he couldn't go to the hospital with her, so he'd made Sharon take him there after school to see her.

Will didn't want a repeat of that adventure. He needed to distract her. "Em, do you remember the name of that squirrel we rescued in Central Park?" he asked.

Emma hiccupped and nodded her head. "Scratchy."

"That's right. How could I forget? Remember how mad your mother was when we brought him home?" Will grinned at Emma. "She was convinced I had rabies."

Emma smiled. "That's cause the crazy thing bit you and scratched your face to pieces."

Will laughed. "Yeah, maybe putting him in a backpack while riding bikes to your place wasn't the smartest idea." He glanced up at Emma as he gently began working the glass from her leg. She was white as a sheet. *Not good.* He needed to keep her talking. "Do you remember what you told me after the great squirrel debacle?" Will asked.

Emma only exhaled a tiny sob.

Will kept talking. "You said you'd still be my friend, even if I had rabies and wasn't pretty anymore."

Emma nodded, a tight smile on her face. "I remember."

"Ta da!" Will grinned up at her and held the tiny piece of glass he'd pulled from her leg triumphantly. "All done."

"Really?" Emma threw her arms around his neck and sobbed. "Thank you," she whispered over and over again as hot tears streaked down her cheeks.

Will held her tight, letting himself inhale the sweet scent of her pretty blonde hair and instantly all their problems melted away. *God, he could hold her forever. Why were some things so easy between them, and others impossible?*

Will pulled Emma close, rubbing her back while she collected herself. He was glad he could help. He knew she'd always been embarrassed by her squeamishness, but it was just one more thing he adored about her. It made her seem more real. Most people didn't get to the see the Emma that Will had fallen for.

To the rest of the world, Emma was a cool, collected, Manhattan fashionista. She always looked flawless and rocked the confidence to match. Every girl wanted to be her and every boy wanted to be with her. But underneath her perfectly poised exterior, Will knew Emma was a sweet girl, with a kind heart, who loved animals, held his hand during scary movies and only felt weak at the sight of blood. And there was a part of him that loved that she needed him when she was scared. Because that was the true fear that had always made Will keep his feelings for Emma at bay. He knew that she didn't need him. And he was terrified that one day she'd figure that out and he'd lose her forever. *Although waiting too long to tell her how he felt had the same effect it seemed.*

Emma's sobs trailed off to a quiet hiccup and she pulled away to glance down at her bloodstained leg. Her bottom lip began to wobble and Will took her face in both his hands. "Don't look, okay? I'm gonna clean it up and then we're going home."

"I can't go home," Emma protested. "Not like this. My father . . . and Tara . . ." Emma groaned. "I got in a fight with her. I said some really awful things."

"Okay, we'll go to my house and let things calm down. You can smooth things over tomorrow, okay?"

Emma nodded.

"Now close your eyes."

She did and Will worked quickly. He poured the rest of his water bottle over the thin cut on Emma's leg. It wasn't deep but it continued to bleed. He slipped his tie off and used it as a makeshift bandage, tying it gently around her leg. "There," he said proudly inspecting his work. "All done. Let's go." He stood up and offered Emma his hand. She took it, but teetered like a fawn with one high heel still on.

Will tried not to smile at her adorableness. Instead, he grabbed her abandoned shoe and scooped her into his arms. "I've got ya, Cinderella."

"Don't call me that. I hate fairytales."

Will smirked. "I know. But I always like the way they end," he said planting a kiss on her forehead.

Emma groaned and buried her face into his neck, which only made Will smile wider. *Maybe today hadn't turned out so bad after all.* He had his princess in his arms and was carrying her home, where she belonged.

18

Emma

WILL CARRIED Emma to his waiting limo. The driver frowned at the sight of her but silently handed Will a blanket and bucket, presumable for her to puke in. And he hadn't been wrong. Emma felt queasy the whole ride home, but she refused to be '*that girl*'. *Girls that puke in limos never get the guy.*

Once Will helped Emma in the car, he slid into the seat next to her and patted his lap for her to lay her head. It might have seemed like an intimate gesture if they hadn't grown up doing it. Emma used to fall asleep with her head in Will's lap gazing up at the sky, dreaming up fashion designs while he edited footage for his next film. Sometimes they'd talk for hours and others they'd sit in silence, just enjoying each other's company. Emma was an only child and Will might as well have been. His brothers were so much older. They were in college before he even started high school.

For a while, Will and Emma had been each other's worlds. Secret keepers, dream chasers and shoulders to cry on. That's what he was offering now. And the torn part of Emma's heart was too tired to resist. But as she lay with her head in Will's lap and he slowly stroked her hair, she couldn't help resenting that he was here for her now, but not when she'd truly needed him. Where was he last year when her parents' divorce had turned ugly? Where was he when they asked her to choose? New York or Boston? Mother over Father? *Sleeping with Liz Vanderveer, that's where.*

Emma let that knowledge settle over her. She didn't think she would ever get over it. But it'd been a year. It was stupid to think Will wouldn't have moved on after Emma left. Besides, they'd never officially been anything more than friends. *Liz had seen to that.* But just because Will hadn't turned into Emma's happily ever after, didn't mean they still couldn't be friends. If anything, tonight proved that Will was still a great guy. He'd rescued her from mortal embarrassment at Cranston's and was making sure she got home safely.

She needed to find a way to let last year go so she could start being Will's friend again. Because truthfully, losing him as a friend had been almost harder than losing the possibility of more. *Besides, how could Emma miss something she'd never had?*

Will

WILL SMIRKED as he stood in his building's elevator with Emma. "Mistletoe seems to keep finding us."

Emma rolled her eyes. "I think you keep looking for it."

Will nudged her with his shoulder. "We can't deny it forever. It's bad Christmas juju."

"Fine," Emma said, taking Will by surprise.

She turned to face him and a lump formed in his throat. *Was Emma really going to kiss him? Shit.* He hadn't thought this through. He didn't want their first kiss to be in an elevator while she was drunk and covered in martinis and blood!

But Emma didn't kiss him. Instead, she raised her hand over her head and glared at the mistletoe. "Here's your holiday high-five. Now leave us alone bad Christmas juju."

Will smiled and met her hand with a solid smack. It made her sway on her feet and he quickly caught her from going down. The elevator doors dinged open and he led her out. "Okay, let's get you home," he said, scooping her up in his arms again.

Emma

IT WAS strange being inside Will's new apartment. It was the same, yet different. Decorated in pale grays and blues, the place still had the same sterile feel as their old apartment. Perhaps that was the reason Emma and Will always chose to hang out at her house when they were younger.

"So this is the new place?" she asked.

"Yep."

"It's nice," she commented. "Big."

Will shrugged. "More like empty. But that means you have five bedrooms to choose from."

"Seriously? Five?" Emma huffed. "My father couldn't even manage a guest room for me."

"Yeah, that's completely foul, Em. But you're more than welcome to stay here next time you're in town."

"I don't think there's gonna be a next time."

"Why not?"

"This whole trip has been a disaster. My father hasn't spent any time with me. All he cares about is Tara and his stupid new family. He doesn't want me anymore."

Will pulled her into a hug. "Only an idiot wouldn't want you, Emma."

She looked up into his deep blue eyes and felt it—that thread of love that had always been there between them. The tether that made her want more, made her want to forgive him for anything. It was thin and frayed, but it was still there and it gave her hope. "Thank you for tonight, Will. For being there."

Will tucked her hair behind her ear, letting his hand linger for a moment too long. "I'm always gonna be there for you, Em."

The way he was looking at her made Emma burn. Will's eyes sparkled with intensity as his thumb brushed her cheek. And that's when it happened. Emma's stomach lurched. She'd been fighting the angry storm of alcohol the whole car ride home. And now, in Will's warm embrace, she was losing the battle. The martinis had worked themselves into a frenzy—they wanted out, and they wanted out now.

Emma pushed Will away violently, her eyes darting frantically around the room. *Bathroom! Where was the bathroom?* She wasn't going to make it. Emma raced to the first option she found and emptied her stomach into the pot of a poor unsuspecting ficus tree.

So it turned out Emma was '*that girl*' after all. Maybe not the girl who puked in the limo, but she had a sneaking suspicion the girl who puked in potted plants was just as doomed in the romance department. Not to mention that she spent the rest of the night on Will's bathroom floor praying to the porcelain gods.

The last thing Emma remembered was pressing her cheek to the cold tile floor as she balled herself up in a fetal position trying to wish the past few days away. She prayed that this was all just a bad dream—that she would wake up in her bed in Boston and shiver away the Christmas break-turned nightmare. But the cataclysmic headache and twitch of her empty stomach told Emma this was real. And no amount of wishing or hoping would take the ache from her heart. Her family was broken for good, and she and Will were hanging on by a thread.

As Emma drifted to sleep, she prayed for a Christmas miracle. Because that was her only hope of turning this holiday around.

Will

WILL WENT to check on Emma again. He hadn't wanted to leave her side, but she'd begged him to give her some privacy between fits of heaving into his toilet. He felt awful for her. Being that kind of sick was the worst. It only happened to Will a handful of times before he learned his alcohol tolerance. Plus, he was an athlete and had an obligation to his team.

Will played lacrosse at St. James Academy, mostly because he was a Taylor and the sport was practically a mandate in his family. But he actually didn't mind. It wasn't his passion, but Will was dedicated enough to the team to keep himself in fighting shape. And that meant hangover free. Which wasn't always easy to do when hanging out with Cranston's crowd.

Luckily, Will's brothers had handed down their secrets of lessening the dreaded post binge-fest hangover. Will had already checked the kitchen to make sure he had all the supplies necessary to make the famous Taylor boys cure-all. Then he'd grabbed a bottle of Pedialyte and two aspirin and headed to his bathroom.

He gently knocked on the door, and when Emma didn't reply, Will pushed it open slightly, revealing Emma asleep on his bathroom floor, her cheek mashed uncomfortably against the white tile. His heart ached for her. She was going through some tough things with her family and he wished there was more he could do. But for the moment, getting her somewhere more comfortable was all he could offer.

Will knelt next to Emma and stroked her hair. "Em, do you want to come to bed?"

She murmured something incoherent and shook her head without opening her eyes.

"Emma. You can't sleep on my bathroom floor. Come on. Let me take you to bed."

"No," she groaned. "Floor good. Moving bad."

Will smirked. *How was she this cute even when she was sloppy drunk?* He shook his head at himself realizing nothing had changed. He was still in love with Emma and would do anything for her—including rescue her from her own stubbornness.

Starting tomorrow, he was going to find a way to help her turn her holiday around. But first things first—he scooped her up and carried her to his bed, propping her up on a bunch of pillows even though she groaned and protested the entire time.

"Just let me sleep, Will."

He opened the Pedialyte and put a straw in it. "Drink this and then you can go to sleep."

She reluctantly took the drink. When she was halfway done he gave her the aspirin. She gulped the pills down and finished the drink, handing it back to him. "Can I please sleep now?"

Will nodded, tucking her in. He turned off the lamp and kissed her head. "Night, Em."

"Will?"

"Yeah?"

"I'm sorry about last year. I really wish we had worked out."

Will froze. *How long had he waited to hear those words?* He stared at Emma, but her eyes had already fluttered closed. He watched the steady rise and fall of her breathing as he tried to calm his emotions. But he found he didn't want to stifle the hope swelling in his chest or the racing of his heart. Emma was the only one who'd ever made him feel that way and it had been so long since he'd let himself even wish for a glimmer of a chance with her. But here she was in his bed, telling him they'd wanted the same thing all along.

That was all he needed to know. He would fight for her. He would let go of last year and all the drama that went with it. If he could focus on the present, focus on Emma, he knew they could get back to the place they had been before everything fell apart. And this time they would work. They had to. Second chances like this didn't come around for no reason.

Will settled himself on the cold leather couch in his room. He knew it was crazy to hope that he and Emma could finally be together. Especially now that she lived in Boston and college was only a few months away. But as Will gazed at Emma's porcelain skin, illuminated by the soft glow of the moonlight filtering in from his windows, he realized it would be even crazier not to try.

19

Emma

EMMA WOKE TO A BLINDING HEADACHE. She blinked the world into focus and took in her strange surroundings. She didn't know where she was and the realization made her panic. She sat up quickly. *Big mistake.* The headache threatened to pull her under as black spots danced in her vision. Emma moved slowly, sliding her legs out from under the covers. The first thing she saw was a gray tie, secured just under her knee. Then the whole humiliating night came crashing back with laser clarity.

She groaned clutching her head. Why was it, the awful and embarrassing times were always so good at implanting themselves in her permanent memory? Emma was certain there was no way she'd forget making a fool of herself at Cranston's party or at Will's apartment. *God, he'd seen her puke last night. And picked glass out of her leg!* Emma glanced down at the tie. It was stained with a tiny spot of deep red. And even though the blood was dry, it still made Emma feel queasy.

She stood up and made her way to the bathroom to wash her face. She nearly screamed when she saw herself in the mirror. Her cheeks were mascara streaked and her hair looked like she'd been through a tornado. She quickly tied up her hair and scrubbed her face clean. It was an improvement, but it did little to make her feel better. Disgrace wasn't something you could wash away. It didn't help that she was still wearing her martini-stained dress from the party either. She could just imagine her father's expression when she did the walk of shame home wearing a ruined party dress. And there was no way he wasn't waiting to berate her for the way she'd spoken to Tara. *Way to go, Emma!*

Sighing, Emma retreated from her reflection to search for Will. She owed him an apology and a giant thank you for taking care of her. As she walked through his room, seeing it clearly for the first time, something caught her eye. The top of his dresser was covered with lacrosse trophies and family photographs. But it was the frame front and center that drew her attention.

Emma picked up the delicate silver frame and let the photograph transport her back to a time when she'd been truly happy. She was sitting with Will under a tree in Central Park. They'd just been to Dylan's Candy Bar and their spoils surrounded them, laid out carefully on Will's school blazer. It was fall, and big orange and yellow maple leaves swirled around them. Will had just thrown an armful of them into the air and Emma was holding a candy apple in one hand, reaching for the leaves with the other. They both must have been laughing wildly, because Emma had never seen herself look so happy. Her fingers caressed the edge of the frame as sorrow filled her heart. *When had she lost it—that happy, carefree love of life?*

"That's my favorite too."

Emma started at the sound of Will's voice. She turned to him, clutching the photo to her chest. "How did you take this?" she asked.

"I had my tripod set up that day. It's a still from the film I shot."

She looked back at the photo, tracing her finger over the strangers in it. "I miss this," she said.

"Me too."

Emma looked at Will. He was staring at her with that smoldering look of his. She hadn't seen him look at her that way in a very long time. *God, what had she said to him last night?* An admission of her feelings tickled her memory, but she couldn't quite put her finger on whether she'd merely thought it or said it out loud. She swallowed hard, shoving her feelings down as she started to put the frame back.

"Keep it," Will said stopping her.

"No, I couldn't. It's yours."

"I'll print another. I want you to have it."

Emma pulled the frame back to her chest and smiled. "Thanks."

"You're welcome."

An awkward silence stretched between them. *Oh, God. She'd said it out loud hadn't she?* Emma resorted to her only plan for such embarrassment—complete and utter avoidance.

"So," she started. "I'd better get out of your hair and let you start your day."

"There's no rush," Will said sitting down on his bed. "How ya feeling?"

Emma sunk down next to him. "I've felt better."

"I'll bet." Will huffed a laugh. "Oh, here." He handed Emma the cup he'd carried into the room. "This will help."

Emma took it, glaring warily at the thick green liquid. She sniffed it and cringed. "Ugh, what is this?"

"Taylor family recipe. Cures any hangover."

"How, by death? It smells awful. There's no way I'm drinking this."

"I promise it works, and it's better than feeling like death all day."

Emma couldn't deny that.

"Drink it, take a shower and you'll feel human again." Will smiled that charming smile of his and Emma was nodding her head before she knew why.

"How's the leg?"

Emma shrugged. "It doesn't really hurt. But I haven't mustered the courage to take the bandage off."

"Well it just so happens Dr. Will is on duty," he teased, pulling Emma's leg onto his lap. "Let's have a look."

She shivered as his warm hands gently steadied her leg and he worked the bandage free. She squeezed her eyes shut, fighting against her quarreling emotions. Emma's stomach roiled with squeamishness, while her heart raced at Will's touch.

"Well, do you want the good news or the bad news?"

Emma's eyes popped open and she stared down at the sluggish green contents of the cup she clutched tightly. It wasn't doing anything to help her queasy stomach. "Good news?" she squeaked.

"You're gonna live. The bad news is the tie wasn't so lucky. I think he's a goner."

"I'm sorry, Will."

"I'm just teasing you. I don't care about a stupid tie. I'm just glad you're okay." He set her leg down and stood. "Just put a Band-Aid on when you get out of the shower. They're under the sink. Towels and everything else you need should be in the linen closet. Feel free to borrow some clothes too. I'll make us some breakfast, while you get cleaned up," he said turning to head out of the room.

"Will?"

He stopped and faced her. "Yeah?"

"Thank you. For everything. For last night . . . and this," she said raising the glass of green sludge.

"Of course."

Emma shook her head. "I mean it. I know you didn't plan to spend your night playing ER doctor to my drunk ass. But I really appreciate it."

"I meant what I said, Emma. I'm always gonna be here for you. You'll see."

Something about the way he said it made hope bubble up in her throat. Will seemed different today. There was a spark of confidence in him she hadn't seen in a while. And she liked it.

"Now don't fall in the shower or I'll be forced to come to your rescue again," he teased, giving her a wolfish grin as he winked and left the room, leaving Emma to ponder Will in endless shower scenarios that made her blush.

Will

WILL WAS PRACTICALLY WHISTLING when he walked into the kitchen, only to be met by Sharon's disappointed gaze. She stood with her arms crossed over her tidy gray and white house staff uniform. "William, do you have something to tell me?"

William? This wasn't good. Sharon only used his full name when he was in big trouble.

"Why yes. You look lovely today, Sharon."

"What happened to the tree, Will?"

"What tree?"

"Lord help me. I don't have time for games, hun. Did you really think I wouldn't notice a missing tree?" she asked pointing to the empty spot where the ficus had once stood.

"Oh, *that* tree. It's the weirdest thing. The tree must've been sick. It threw up last night. I've never seen a tree do that before, so I figured it wasn't a good sign and I got it out of the house before it infected the other plants."

"William Michael Taylor, I'm not playing. Your mother's not going to be pleased when she finds out you killed her ficus. You know how much she loves her stupid plants."

Will snorted because it was true. His mother probably talked to her damn plants more than she did to him. *That is, when she bothered to be home.* "She'd have to be here to notice it was missing, Sharon."

"Will." Sharon walked around the counter and put a hand on his shoulder. "What's going on with you, hun? Talk to me."

Will sighed. He should've known better than to think he could get away with it. Sharon was like a bloodhound. He knew she wouldn't quit until she dragged the truth out of him, so he figured he'd just fess up and save himself some time.

He walked over to the hall closet and pulled the tree out. It was still in the large trash bag he'd slid under the pot last night. It looked sad with the bag tied to its gnarled trunk.

"I brought a girl home last night and she threw up in the ficus. I was gonna go get a new tree today before anyone noticed."

Sharon was staring at the tree with mild amusement. "Seven bathrooms in this apartment and your girl throws up in a plant? You sure know how to pick 'em, hun."

Will was grinning now, too. "Yeah, probably not Emma's finest moment."

Sharon's jaw dropped. "It was Emma?" Will watched as she morphed from motherly to giddy schoolgirl in a blink of an eye. "As in *your* Emma?" Sharon asked. "She's in New York?"

Will blushed, rubbing his hand over the back of his neck. "Yeah, but can you keep it down? She's still here."

Sharon lowered her voice, losing some of her giddiness. "She spent the night?"

"Not like that. She just needed a place to crash."

"What happened?"

"Nothing yet."

Sharon clapped her hands together practically bouncing on her toes.

Will sighed. "Sharon, we're just friends."

She barked a laugh. "And reindeer can fly!"

"Sharon, please don't . . ."

"Will, this is the chance you've been waiting for. I know you've always wanted to be more than friends with that girl. She's the one for you. You know it. I know it. Now it's time you make sure Emma knows it."

"Christ, Sharon. Can you please be cool about this? This is the first time we've talked in a year. I can't just blurt out, I love you."

"Why not?"

"This isn't one of the romantic comedies you make me watch. It doesn't work like that in real life."

"William—"

"Sharon, please let me handle this."

"Fine, fine." Sharon made the sign of the cross over her heart. "I'll be cool. But don't screw this up. I don't want to see you devastated again like you were when she moved."

"Me either."

Sharon patted his cheek. "You don't always get second chances in life, hun. Don't take that for granted."

"I'm not. I was about to cook her breakfast."

"In my kitchen?" Sharon's hands were on her hips. "Do you want this girl to fall in love with you?"

"Yes."

"Then maybe you should let me do the cooking."

"I can cook," Will replied indignantly.

"Since when?"

Will huffed. "I think I can manage bacon and eggs."

Sharon didn't look as though she shared Will's confidence. But after a silent standoff, she sighed and went to the fridge to take out a packet of bacon and the carton of eggs.

"Sharon, I can do it." Will protested. "Stop hovering."

"I don't hover. I'm not one of those chopper parents."

"It's helicopter parent," Will said grinning.

Sharon always tried to keep up with what she thought was current teen lingo, even though most of the time it made her sound ridiculous. But it only made Will love her even more, because at least she cared enough to try, which was more than he could say for his parents. Sharon's warmth and sunny personality was an eternal brightness in Will's life, and he honestly didn't know what he would do without her. It was because of Sharon that he had a moral compass at all.

Will kissed the top of Sharon's head. "I know you're not hovering. But I want to do this for Emma. It won't mean as much if you cook her breakfast. I'm trying to show her I care."

Sharon squeezed Will's hand, smiling. "You are turning into a fine man, William."

"I learned from the best."

20

Emma

WILL WAS RIGHT—THAT slimy green drink was magical. Emma felt a million times better after slurping it down and taking a hot shower. She towel dried her hair and threw it into a messy bun, then went in search of something to wear. Will's lacrosse hoodie caught her eye. It hung on the back of his door. Her heart twisted a bit as she walked over to it and pulled it down. Holding the soft cotton filled her with familiar longing.

For years Emma had yearned to be the girl who got to wear Will's jersey. She knew it was ridiculous. She didn't need to be branded with his number to feel confident in their relationship. But when she'd seen the other players' girlfriends wearing them, she couldn't stave off the sudden pang of jealousy. It was one of the first times she knew she truly wanted to be Will's.

Emma ran her fingers over the hoodie. It wasn't his lacrosse jersey, but it was pretty damn close. She slipped the large gray hoodie over her head. It was warm and soft, falling to her mid thighs. She let her towel drop beneath it, feeling a bit ridiculous at the thrill that rushed through her. *Get a grip, Emma. It's just a hoodie.*

She pulled open Will's top drawer and stared at rows of neatly folded boxers and socks. Her cheeks burned. *This was not how she imagined seeing Will's underwear for the first time.* She grabbed a pair and slipped them on before she lost her nerve. She had to roll them at her narrow waist to get them to stay up, virtually making them disappear under the oversized hoodie. *Great, she looked like she wasn't wear anything at all under the bulky sweatshirt.* But pawing through more of Will's drawers for a better option didn't appeal to her. This already felt like an invasion of his privacy. *God, why couldn't just one of Will's five siblings have been a girl so she could be borrowing her clothes right now?*

Emma grabbed a pair of warm wool socks and pulled them on. They went almost to her knees, stopping just short of the Band-Aid on her left leg. She averted her eyes from the innocent looking bandage. There was no sign of blood, but just looking at the Band-Aid made her remember the gory scene the broken martini glasses had caused last night. Emma shuddered. She'd be happy if she never saw a martini ever again. She couldn't believe she'd been stupid enough to let Marcy convince her drinking and dancing could solve all her problems.

Grumbling, Emma mentally revised her blog post again.

A Haute Chic's Holiday Survival Guide

1. *Martinis are mercurial.*
2. *Dancing is a dangerous distraction.*
3. *Sometimes white knights deserve a second chance.*

A ONCE OVER in the mirror made Emma frown. Baggy hoodie, tall socks and shower hair—not her best look. *But did it really matter?* Will was just being a good friend; nothing more. And Emma had promised herself that she'd try to find a way to be his friend too. She at least owed him that after everything he'd done to help her last night. She took a deep breath and walked out of his room.

Emma followed the smell of bacon and coffee to the kitchen, her empty stomach rumbling. The sight of Will, washed golden in the warm morning sunlight, made her stop in her tracks. He was flipping pieces of bacon in a pan, holding a mug of coffee in his other hand. The scene was so domestic it hurt her heart. On one hand it was everything she ever wanted with Will. Cozy mornings together, cooking breakfast and talking over coffee. On the other, it was everything she'd had with her family, and lost.

Will

WILL LOOKED up and saw Emma staring at him. He was tempted to pinch himself, but a pop of hot bacon grease did the trick for him. If it hadn't been for the sting of reality he might have thought he was dreaming. Because there was Emma, standing in his kitchen wearing his lacrosse hoodie—looking sexy as hell. She might as well have stepped right out of one Will's fantasies.

He couldn't find words. He just stood their gaping at her, while she smiled. Another pop of grease stung his arm and he hissed.

"Need some help?" Emma asked sidling up next to him at the stove.

"Oh, uh sure. Do you want some coffee?"

"I'd love some."

Will turned away from the stove to pour her a mug of coffee. He took a deep breath trying to collect himself. He hadn't expected Emma to be wearing *that* when she came out of his room. Never before had he thought of his large gray sweatshirt as sexy. But the way Emma was wearing it certainly was. And it threw him off his game.

When he returned to the stove with her coffee Emma was stirring the eggs. "One coffee, no cream, three sugars."

Emma grinned taking the cup and nudging him playfully in the shoulder. "You remember how I like my coffee?"

"I remember everything about you," he replied, nudging her back.

They stood side-by-side at the stove, Emma stirring the eggs, while Will flipped the bacon. He watched Emma out of the corner of his eye. Each time her soft lips touched her coffee mug, he wanted to kiss her. And each time her elbow grazed his, he wanted to take her in his arms and hoist her onto the counter so she could wrap her legs around him and never let go.

She turned and said something to him, but he didn't hear her over the fantasies running through his head. Emma put her hand on his arm, startling him back to reality.

"Will?" She was staring at him with concern.

"Hmm?"

"Do you smell something burning?"

He did. Come to think of it, the kitchen seemed a bit smoky. His brain finally found focus. "Shit! The toast." He'd forgotten about it completely. He'd put it in the toaster right before Emma walked into the kitchen.

Will whirled around to the back counter, ejecting four black pieces of bread from the toaster. They were smoking and burnt to a crisp. Emma came over to inspect them and when Will held up the plate of pathetic toast they both burst into laughter.

Sharon chose that moment to waltz into the kitchen. "Okay, I said you could use my kitchen, Will. But not at the expense of burning it down. What's going on in here?"

Will held out the plate of charred bread to Sharon. "Toast?"

She shook her head, but an amused smile lit her face. "Alright you two, new plan. I cook, you eat. Okay?"

"I think that's a good plan," Emma replied trying to stifle her giggles.

"Emma, you remember Sharon," Will said, surprisingly nervous at reintroducing the two most important women in his life to each other.

"Of course," Emma said holding her hand out. "It's good to see you, Sharon."

Sharon looked surprised by Emma's manners. Most Manhattaner's didn't shake hands with the help. "And you as well," Sharon replied, giving Will a sly, but pleased, glance.

Will led Emma to the barstools on the other side of the cooktop kitchen island. He watched as she sipped her coffee, chatting easily with Sharon, who tried to rescue their breakfast. Will couldn't help but smile as he watched Emma and Sharon converse. It unlocked something within him and the hollowness that normally plagued him dimmed a bit more. Suddenly, his house didn't feel so empty.

21

Emma

In a matter of minutes Sharon somehow revived the half-burnt breakfast Will had been preparing. She served them deliciously greasy breakfast sandwiches on croissants piled high with bacon, eggs and cheese, before making a plate for herself.

Sharon threw Will a warm smile when she was done. “Now don’t think this means you’re getting out of doing these dishes, hun.”

Will grinned. “I wouldn’t dream of it.”

Sharon winked at him and sashayed out of the room, taking her plate with her.

“She’s so sweet,” Emma said once they were alone.

“You only say that because she likes you.”

“How do you know she likes me?”

“She still made you breakfast after I told her you puked on the ficus tree.”

"Oh my God, you didn't!" Emma groaned, covering her face with her hands.

Will gently pried them away but he couldn't hide his laughter and it only made Emma's cheeks burn hotter.

"Will!" she whined. "I can't believe you told her I did that."

"Relax. I've done way worse. Besides, Sharon said she'd cover for us as long as I replace the tree before my mother gets back."

"Ugh, I still feel like an idiot."

Will tugged on a loose piece of hair that escaped Emma's bun. "Yeah, but you're a cute idiot."

She rolled her eyes at him. "Seriously, tell me how much I owe you for the tree. The least I can do is pay for it."

"I don't know . . . I kinda like the idea of you owing me," Will teased, snagging a piece of bacon off of her plate.

Was it her imagination or was Will flirting with her? She needed to change the subject. So far things were going well between them, and if Emma was going to make this *'friends'* thing work she needed to avoid flirtation territory.

"So, how long do we have to replace the tree before your parents get home?" she asked hoping to stay on a safe subject.

Will shrugged.

"Where are they anyway?"

"Who knows? Bali? Bangladesh? Botswana?" He replied sounding bitter.

"Do they only visit places that start with the letter B?" Emma asked trying to lighten the mood.

"No, but I can't keep track. I usually just pick a letter and start naming destinations until Sharon stops me."

"Do they really travel that much?" Emma asked.

"Yep."

"But they'll be home for Christmas, right?"

"Honestly, I'm starting to think they might not." Will sighed. "I've sorta been in denial about it."

"About what?"

"Them ditching me. I mean I know I wasn't *'planned',*" he said using air quotes. "The six year age gap between me and my brothers is pretty obvious, but I guess I didn't know how desperate my parents were to be done parenting."

Emma's heart faltered. Will looked so sad that she had the sudden urge to leap into his arms and kiss away every last trace of frown disgracing his perfect lips. *Friend zone, Emma. Keep it in the friend zone!*

She sighed, shaking her head. "Parents suck."

"I'll drink to that," Will said raising his coffee mug.

Emma pretended to shiver. "Don't say the word drink." And she was pleased to see it brought Will's easy smile back to his face. "When did Christmas become such a crappy holiday?"

Will only shrugged.

Emma sighed. *What was wrong with their parents? Couldn't they see how messed up everything was?* She sipped her coffee seriously hoping Will's parents wouldn't ditch him for the holidays. It was obviously bothering him, and as she looked around his enormously empty home, she could see why.

Emma didn't know Will's parents that well. She'd only met them a handful of times at functions or galas when she used to live in the city, but it's not as though she had meaningful conversations with them. They seemed nice enough. Certainly not like the type of people to abandon their son on Christmas. But then again, Emma was learning that it was hard to ever really know someone. And parents were no exception.

She decided the best thing she could do for Will was to let him vent if he wanted to. She knew it would've made her feel a lot better if she could rant about her father's shortcomings to someone who understood. Emma swiveled toward Will on her barstool and stole a crumb of bacon from his plate. "Well, you're not alone if that makes you feel any better. I'll be having a crappy Christmas right next door."

Will huffed a laugh. "Thanks, but that doesn't really help."

"I know. It just sounds pathetic, doesn't it?"

"Yeah, we really should do something about that."

"Like what?" Emma asked.

Will scratched his chin, thinking for a moment. "What was your favorite part of Christmas when you were a kid?" he asked.

"Probably Christmas dinner. My parents would stay home all day and we'd cook for hours. Ham and homemade mashed potatoes and every type of cookie I could dream of. I just remember my parents laughing so much." Emma was quiet for a moment, holding onto the memory. "What about you? What's your favorite part?"

"Okay, so I know it's kinda silly, but we have this family tradition where every year we drive to Emmerich Tree Farm upstate and pick out our Christmas tree. We cut it down and everything."

Emma laughed. "How very Griswold."

"We've been doing it since I was born. When I was really little, my brothers used to let me ride on their shoulders so I could scout for the best tree. And when I got older we would play hide and seek in the trees and have snowball fights. Oh and the apple cider is the best thing ever!"

Will's blue eyes seemed to glow from within as he reminisced about his holiday tradition. It made Emma's heart ache. She wished she could give him that kind of Christmas again. Or anything that would keep his eyes that bright.

Will ran a hand through his messy hair. "I know I'm almost eighteen, but I was sorta looking forward to having one last trip to Emmerich's." He shrugged. "I'm not ready to give it up yet, ya know?"

Emma nodded. *She did know.* She'd been looking forward to one more Christmas in New York with her father. It wasn't fair. Everything would be changing soon. Graduation and college were looming around the corner, and she was excited for what the future could bring, but the inevitable change made her want to cling to the familiarity of childhood even more. Just like Will, Emma was still hoping to get this one last holiday to be a kid again.

Renewed determination flared in Emma's chest. "Maybe we can still save our holidays. Mine, not so much, since hell will probably freeze over before my parents share a meal together again, but we could still go up to that Christmas tree farm and get your tree."

Will smiled sadly and reached over to squeeze her hand. "Emma, I love you for trying, but it's probably time I let it go." He stood up and began clearing their dishes. "It hasn't been the same since my brothers stopped coming anyway."

Emma knew how much Will missed them. She even missed them. Well at least she missed Gabe. Emma had Will's brother Gabe to thank for their friendship. It wasn't until Gabe went off to college that she and Will had become inseparable. Will was desperately lonely without Gabe around, prompting him to practically become Emma's shadow. But she hadn't minded. Especially since that was also when she first became aware that she hoped one day she and Will could be more than friends.

Emma stood, trying to shake away those not so distant feelings for Will. She rounded the island to help him with the dishes praying she could keep her heart in check.

She dried while he washed. "Ya know," Emma started, when the silence had stretched out between them. "If you're desperate for brother time, I have a super annoying one next door. You can borrow him anytime."

"Colin?" Will smirked. "That kid's awesome."

Emma frowned. "Um, there's no way you're talking about the Dothraki-speaking pain in the ass who stole my bedroom."

Will's laugh rumbled through Emma as he handed her a dish to dry. "That's the one."

She rolled her eyes.

"Aw, come on, Em. You just gotta give the kid a chance," Will said, bumping his hip into hers.

"Easy for you to say. He's not your brother."

"I'd love to have him as a little brother. He's a riot. And hella smart, too."

"More like hella weird," she grumbled.

"That's just because you don't speak boy."

"I speak boy just fine, thank you very much. It's dorky insta-brother I have a problem with."

"Well *I'd* love to have an insta-little brother."

Emma blinked up at Will, startled by the honesty in his sparkling blue eyes. "Why?" she asked.

"I've always wanted a little brother. You get to sculpt his little mind and introduce him to the world. Plus, you get to be a super hero to him, Em. That kid's gonna look up to you for everything."

Will's words filled Emma with guilt. She hadn't thought of it like that. She hadn't even given Colin a chance. None of this was his fault. Plus, how could she shirk him off when she'd been him. She remembered how desperately she'd wanted siblings when she was his age. It was lonely being an only child. It was obvious that Tara wasn't the warm and fuzzy type. And Emma knew from experience her father wasn't either. From what Emma could tell, it seemed like Hodor was Colin's only friend, and that did not bode well for his future.

Words were tumbling out of Emma's mouth before she could stop them. "Do you think you could help me with Colin?"

"What do you mean?"

"You're right. I don't know how to talk to him. All he does is watch cartoons or ask me to play in his room. I don't know how to relate to that. But I don't want to be an awful sister."

Will smiled. "All any kid wants is someone to spend time with them."

"So . . . just do stuff with him?"

Will nodded.

"But what kind of stuff?"

"He's from South Carolina, right?"

"Yeah. So what?"

"So, this is his first Christmas in New York. Show him how great our city is."

"Like take him ice skating or on a sleigh ride through the park?"

"Yes, he'd love that."

"You think?"

"Hell, I'd love that."

Emma toyed with the too long sleeve of her borrowed lacrosse hoodie. "Would you . . . maybe wanna come with us?"

Will looked up from the dishes, a sly smile on his handsome face. "Are you asking me out, Emma?" he asked nudging her with his elbow.

She nudged him right back. "No, I'm asking you to help me get to know my little brother."

Will grinned. "I'd love to."

"Great. How about tomorrow, when I'm less hung over?"

"It's a date."

22

Emma

Emma slipped quietly into her father's sleek white apartment and released a sigh when it appeared she was alone. She hadn't been looking forward to explaining where she'd been all night or why she was dressed like a lacrosse player's chew toy. But then again, that would require her father noticing her—*something that hadn't happened since she'd returned to New York.*

Still, Emma had expected Tara would've told her father how terribly she'd reacted to babysitting Colin, prompting another, "be a team player," lecture from him. She tugged the hem of Will's oversized hoodie down further, but it did little to improve her appearance. She still looked like she wasn't wearing anything underneath thanks to the shortness of his rolled boxers. She made her way over to corner where her luggage rested sadly in a pile. She dug through her clothes until she found a pair of pajamas and then scurried to the bathroom to change.

Emma swapped Will's underwear for a pair of her own only to feel immediately embarrassed about what to do with them. *Did she return them? Keep them? Burn them? Ugh . . . why did she still have these feelings for him?* It made everything so much more complicated.

She tugged on a pair of red plaid pajama pants, letting the worn-soft material comfort her. Emma looked at her reflection in the mirror. She'd intended to change into her own top, but as she stared at herself in Will's hoodie she couldn't seem to find the strength to take it off. It was so warm and cozy and . . . Will. It smelled like him, or rather his Valentino cologne—a mixture of sage and mandarin, with a hint of spice. Emma was addicted to the smell and all the desire it conjured. She inhaled deeply. *God, how she'd missed that smell.*

Two days ago, even the faintest whiff of it would have filled her with anger and regret. But now . . . well now it gave Emma a feeling that frightened her even more—hope.

Will

WILL COULDN'T STOP GRINNING. Things were going better than he'd hoped. He already had a date with Emma, when all he'd been aiming for was a full day without a fight. Today they'd managed breakfast, dishes and conversation without arguing or any mention of the dreaded winter formal. That was major progress.

He stepped onto the elevator on his way to meet the delivery guys with the new ficus Sharon had located. When the doors dinged closed, Will glanced up. The mistletoe was merrily swaying above his head and for once, it didn't seem to be taunting him. Will felt his heart warm as he thought about all the times he'd ended up under it with Emma in the past few days. He believed in signs and this was a good one.

Emma

EMMA WAS deep in her hangover movie marathon when she heard the keys jingle in the apartment door. Colin came bounding in with Hodor on his heels.

"Emma's home! Emma's home!" he shrieked practically tackling her where she sat on the couch.

"Colin, honey, inside voices please," Tara called from the kitchen. "And remember what we said about personal space?"

Colin's happy face immediately crumpled as he slid off of Emma, moving to the far corner of the couch. "Sorry," he mumbled.

"It's okay," Emma replied, trying to remember why she thought subjecting herself to an entire day with Colin was a good idea.

"Cool shirt," Colin remarked. "My friend Will has the same one."

Emma couldn't hide her smile. "Yeah, I know."

Tara came into the living room, arching a perfect eyebrow at Emma's rumpled appearance as she noted the lacrosse hoodie. Emma stared right back, daring Tara to say something. She had no right to judge what boys Emma spent her time with after ruining her parents' marriage.

Tara seemed to catch Emma's hostility and wisely, her only comment was to Colin. "Honey, why don't you leave Emma alone? You're disrupting her movie."

Colin pouted, but started to move from the couch.

"Actually, Tara," Emma said staring directly at her aloof

soon-to-be step-mother. "I was going to ask if I could take Colin out to the park tomorrow."

Tara looked startled. "Really?"

"That is, if you want to go?" Emma asked looking at Colin.

"Best idea ever!" he exclaimed leaping back onto the couch to throw his arms around her neck.

Emma laughed. "I guess that's a yes?"

"Definitely yes!"

"Good. It's a date."

Colin clapped his hands and bounced up and down, sending Hodor into a barking fit.

"Okay, okay. That's enough excitement, Colin. Why don't you go wash up for dinner. It'll be here soon." Tara waited until Colin darted out of the living room before turning to Emma. "We ordered dinner from Café China. I didn't know you'd be home. Would you like me to call back and add to our order?"

Emma grabbed another slice of pizza from the box she'd ordered when her stomach began rumbling a few hours ago. "Nope. I took care of myself. But thanks," she added without sincerity, since it was obvious that Tara had forgotten to consider Emma in the family dinner plans. *So much for one big happy family,* she thought bitterly.

"Will my father be home for dinner?" Emma asked.

Tara smiled tightly. "He's working late. And Teddy and I usually go out for a late dinner once Colin is in bed."

Emma snorted. *Of course they did. Why would her father change his usual dinner plans with his precious Tara to spend any time with his daughter?*

Tara twisted her hands uncomfortably. "Would you like me to ask him to come home for dinner instead? I know he's been busy, but I'm sure—"

"Don't bother," Emma interrupted. She turned back to face the television, done discussing her father with her mother's shiny new replacement.

Tara tentatively took a step closer. "Emma? Thank you for inviting Colin out with you tomorrow. It means a great deal to your father and I that you get along."

Emma glared at Tara. "I'm not doing it for you." And for the first time, Emma truly meant it. Colin deserved better parents just as much as Emma did. She turned back to face the television until Tara got the hint that the conversation was over. After a moment, Emma heard the sound of Tara's heels clacking down the hall, then the quiet click of her bedroom door.

Emma let out a breath and squeezed her eyes shut, silently praying for the strength to somehow turn this holiday around . . . for all their sakes.

23

Emma

Emma was woken bright and early by sloppy dog kisses. She grumbled and swatted the slobbery golden retriever away, stretching her stiff limbs. She rubbed the sleep out of her eyes and was startled to find Colin standing inches from her face.

"You're up! She's up, Mom!"

Emma groaned. She was not a morning person, and a screeching seven-year old was doing nothing to change that fact.

"Are you ready to go, Emma?" Colin asked with excitement.

"Huh?"

"To the park. Remember, yesterday you said we could go."

"I remember, but I didn't mean at . . ." she looked around. "What time is it?"

"The time in New York is 7:43 am," Penelope's disembodied

voice replied through the hidden speakers. Emma cringed. She'd never be able to get used to that.

"The park's open," Colin replied. "I checked."

Emma rolled her eyes. "Of course it's open. It's a park. They're always open."

"Actually, there are over 1700 parks in New York City and only forty-six percent of them are open to the public twenty-four hours a day, 365 days a year."

Emma groaned. *Was this kid serious?*

Tara walked into the living room at that moment giving Emma a sympathetic look. She was dressed to impress, carrying a Prada handbag and a stunning red and black Louis Vuitton tartan fur coat over her arm. "Colin, what did I tell you?"

"I didn't wake her up, Mom. I swear." Colin grinned like a fiend at Emma and spoke in a conspiratorial whisper. "Mom said I couldn't wake you up, but she didn't say Hodor couldn't."

Emma sighed. "It's fine. I was getting up anyway."

"Are you still heading to the park?" Tara asked tentatively.

"Of course!" Colin interjected, but Tara ignored him, waiting for Emma's answer.

"Yeah," Emma replied glancing back at Colin, who looked like he might explode with excitement. "Anything I need to know . . . like allergies or I don't know . . . kid stuff?"

Tara smiled. "No, he's your typical seven-year old. Full of energy and questions." She dug her wallet out of her purse and handed Emma a stack of bills and a credit card. "Here, this should cover any expenses today."

Emma stared at the cash. *Expenses? Did Tara think they were taking a private jet to the park?*

"Oh, and you don't have to bring Hodor to the park. The dog walker will be by to take him out at noon."

"Right," Emma said looking at the happy dog that Colin was currently wrestling. She hadn't even thought about Hodor, but was suddenly grateful she wouldn't have to wrangle the dog *and* Colin on their outing.

Tara swept across the room and gave Colin a kiss on the head. "Be good, honey. And listen to Emma. She's in charge, okay?"

"Okay, Mom. Love you."

"You too, sweetie." Then Tara was breezing out the door. "You two have fun."

When the door clicked shut Emma suddenly felt fear coil in her gut. *What the hell had she been thinking?* She was in *way* over her head. She didn't know anything about kids. Or dogs. She'd never babysat and never had a pet. This did not bode well for their day.

Colin was already tugging on her arm. "Come on, Emma. Let's go to the park!"

"Okay, but I need to get dressed first." *And a shower would be nice,* she thought wistfully. But she doubted Colin's patience would last that long. "Can you watch TV while I get ready?"

"Okay, but hurry up. I want to see the whole park!"

Emma dragged her suitcase into the guest bathroom and groaned. She didn't exactly pack park-hiking attire. Luckily she'd worn her Frye ankle boots trudging through the Boston snow on her way to the train station. She pawed through her clothes, pulling out black leggings and a gray cashmere sweater. They'd have to do. With her red Burberry jacket and ivory scarf she was confident she could pull off the look. Her hair, on the other hand, was a different story. Emma looked in the mirror and groaned. "Make it work," she said, quoting her favorite '*Project Runway*' mentor.

She ran a brush through her tangled blonde hair, piling it on top of her head in a stylish messy bun before washing her face. She was just brushing her teeth when she heard a knock at the bathroom door. *Really? She'd only been in the bathroom for three minutes!*

"Just a minute," Emma mumbled spitting and rinsing toothpaste from her mouth in a hurry.

There was another knock at the door and Emma swore under her breath. *Why the hell had she thought this was a good idea?*

Will. That's why.

She cursed him and his adorable smile as she grabbed the door handle and yanked it open resisting the urge to strangle Colin. But Colin wasn't standing there.

"Will!" she exclaimed, drinking in his gorgeous features as he leaned against the doorframe, smirking at her with that damn smile of his.

"Hello, gorgeous," he greeted.

Emma looked down at herself, still in pajama pants and his hoodie. Meanwhile, Will looked like he'd just stepped out of a magazine. *How was it possible to look that good this early?*

"Um, hi," she mumbled. "I thought you were Colin."

Will grinned. "Nope, but you should probably tell him not to let strangers in the house."

"Oh. Right." Emma scratched her head feeling flustered with Will staring at her so intently.

He took a step closer and his intoxicating cologne filled the bathroom, flooding her with longing. Emma felt lightheaded as Will reached up, pressing a finger to the corner of her mouth. Her breath hitched and she closed her eyes at his touch. But he didn't linger.

"You missed a spot," he said, smirking at her when she opened her eyes.

Emma glanced in the mirror to see a smudge of toothpaste still clinging to her face, right where Will had touched her. Her cheeks burned with embarrassment. This was not how she wanted to start her day with Will. He was too used to seeing her like this—casual and messy. It was no wonder she'd never moved out of the friend zone.

Emma sighed as she wiped the toothpaste away. "Thanks. I was rushing to get ready. I didn't realize Colin wanted to go to the park at the crack of dawn."

"You told him about the park last night?"

"Yeah."

Will laughed. "I'm surprised he slept at all."

"Are all kids early risers?"

"Do you *not* remember Christmas morning?"

"Yeah, but that was Christmas. This is just the park."

Will gave Emma a knowing smile. "That's the beauty of little brothers. The idea of spending time with you is like Christmas morning to them."

Emma was speechless and thankfully Will seemed to catch her bewilderment.

"Take your time getting ready. Colin and I are going to make breakfast."

Emma raised her eyebrows. "Should I call Sharon?"

He laughed. "I think I can handle bagels and cream cheese."

"If you say so."

Emma started to shut the door but Will stopped her. "I'm glad you're still wearing it."

"What?"

"My lacrosse hoodie."

Emma felt her skin burn with delight. "Oh."

"I meant to tell you yesterday, you look better in it than I ever imagined."

Her cheeks turned scarlet. "Thanks."

"I think I could get used to seeing you in it." Will gave her a wink. "I'll save you a bagel."

Emma watched him walk away with a dumbfounded expression on her face and a tornado of butterflies in her stomach. When she finally found the strength to shut the bathroom door, she gazed at her reflection, hugging her arms tight around the hoodie she wore. *So he'd thought about her wearing it too? Did it mean the same thing to him as it did to her? And did that change things between them?*

Will

WILL SAT NEXT to Emma while Colin scrambled about the limo looking out the windows and pointing at the buildings he knew. So far the date was going well. *If this really was a date.*

Will figured there was no harm in pretending it was until Emma told him otherwise. Of course taking a seven-year-old on a first date wasn't exactly how he'd pictured winning Emma over. But strangely there was something perfect about it. Colin's light energy was infectious and it kept Will and Emma from slipping into the problems of their past or visiting any of the heavier issues they were having with their parents.

Plus, Will couldn't deny how much he loved being Emma's crutch. She was truly helpless when it came to dealing with kids. Will thought it was adorable when she tried to tie Colin's shoes as they were getting ready to leave the apartment. Colin had looked up at Emma and said, "I'm seven, I know how to tie my shoes."

Emma merely looked at Will with pure desperation, to which he immediately swooped in and rescued her with a joke. "That was your first little brother test, Colin. You were right, Emma, he passed. Looks like I owe you a hot chocolate."

Colin had exclaimed that he wanted a hot chocolate too, and Will assured him that Emma was going to take them both to her favorite top secret hot chocolate shop, which was where they were presently headed.

The driver stopped outside of Jacques Torres Chocolate on

Amsterdam Avenue and Colin squealed with delight. "Are we going in there?" he asked drooling over the decadent storefront.

Emma nodded. "Yep."

Colin squealed again and threw his arms around Emma's neck. "Best day ever!"

She laughed. "Wait until you taste the chocolate."

When they arrived at the counter, Will gave the barista a wink and introduced Colin. The peppy barista didn't disappoint. With her hands on her hips, she cheerfully addressed Colin. "You wouldn't happen to be Emma Rhode's little brother, would you?"

Stunned speechless for a change, Colin nodded.

"Well, why didn't you say so?" the barista challenged. "I've got our secret table reserved for you."

The girl led Will, Emma and Colin to a small marble table tucked away behind the mirrored pillars. "Wait right here and I'll be back with your special order," she said.

Colin gazed open-mouthed at the glass cases surrounding them. They were filled with chocolates and truffles and cookies. It was clear he was impressed. And from the look on Emma's face, so was she.

"When did you have time to arrange this?" she whispered to Will.

He smiled coyly and shrugged, like he didn't know what she was talking about. In reality, he'd spent the entire day yesterday setting up little scenes like this to make Emma and Colin's day perfect. And the glowing smiles on both their faces at the moment made it all worth it.

The barista returned a few minutes later with three mugs of hot chocolate and a tray full of goodies. "Three triple fudge brownie cocoa's," she said setting the tray down on their table.

Colin's eyes were as big as saucers when he saw the array of cookies and truffles that accompanied the hot chocolates. "Are those all for us?"

The barista knelt down, lowering her voice. “These are from our secret recipe vault. We don’t usually share these with just anybody, but since you’re a friend of Emma’s . . .”

“I’m her brother,” Colin said proudly.

The barista winked and tousled Colin’s corn silk hair. “That’s why you’re getting the royal treatment.”

Emma glanced over Colin’s head and mouthed ‘thank you’ to Will and suddenly his heart felt too big for his chest. As he watched her beaming at Colin, pointing out her favorite chocolates, he realized he’d do just about anything to keep that smile on her face.

24

Emma

BY THE TIME they left Jacques, Colin was so hopped up on sugar that Will suggested they go ice skating to work off some of his energy. They walked through Central Park toward Wollman Rink. Colin ran up ahead while Will stayed close to Emma's side. She couldn't keep the smile from her face as the crisp winter air stung her cheeks. The park looked especially beautiful today. There'd been a light dusting of snow overnight and it still clung to the ground, making the gentle hills of Central Park glisten in the morning light. The trees they passed under shimmered with a layer of frost, their thin, brittle limbs twinkling like chandeliers made of the finest crystal.

Emma found herself shivering at the beauty. Will moved closer, mistaking her tremor for a chill. But Emma didn't protest when he put his arm around her, rubbing her arm vigorously for warmth. And she definitely didn't mind when he decided to leave his arm wrapped neatly around her waist. It certainly wasn't just his body heat that was driving up her temperature. Being so close to Will made Emma feel like she could scorch the park with just one touch.

She snuck a peek at him from under her lashes to find he was already staring at her, the beginnings of a smile tugging at the corner of his gorgeous lips. It nearly stole Emma's frozen breath right from her lungs.

"Have I told you how beautiful you look today?" Will asked.

Emma stopped walking. She stared into Will's blue eyes, finding only brutal honesty there. He took her gloved hand and pulled her closer. She fought her nerves and moved closer still, only stopping when their chests were pressed together. They shared a frozen breath, white swirls of steam dancing in the air between them. *This was it. Will was going to kiss her.* And from the frantic pumping of her heart, Emma realized that she wanted him to.

Emma reached her hand up, letting her frozen fingers touch Will's cheek. He leaned into it, the warmth of his skin stinging even through her gloves.

"Em . . ." Will started. But if he'd been about to say something else she didn't hear it. Instead her cheek was met with a solid *whack!*

Emma yelped, stumbling back. Both she and Will looked at each other, stunned for a moment. But then Colin's laughter filled the air.

"Gotcha!" he yelled, hurling another snowball in their direction.

"Oh, it's on!" Will called back, pulling Emma behind a tree for cover as he set to packing together a few lumpy snowballs.

Emma was still clutching her cheek from where Colin's first snowball had hit her. "Is it normal that I want to kill him?" she muttered.

Will grinned and handed Emma a snowball. "I knew you'd

get the hang of this sibling thing."

Emma narrowed her eyes. "He's not gonna know what hit him." Then she stepped out from behind the tree and hurled a snowball at Colin. She was a terrible shot and missed him completely. But his shriek of joy was almost as satisfying as if she'd pelted him. She dashed after Colin, who dropped his snowball and ran. Will followed behind, bombarding them both with snowballs.

"Hey! Whose side are you on?" Emma called.

"Let's get him!" Colin yelled, and before Emma knew it, she and the bubbly little boy were crouched behind a shrub, chucking snowballs at Will. It was completely useless. Will had much better aim, so she hatched a plan to beat him playing to her strengths. Emma whispered her plan to Colin who grinned like a maniac. Two seconds later he fell to the side clutching his leg and started to wail.

"Will! Will! Help. Colin's hurt."

Will sprinted to her side. "What happened?" he asked worry in his voice as he surveyed Colin's leg. "Buddy, tell me where it hurts."

"Here!" Colin said springing up to tackle Will. He was able to bowl Will over from his crouching position easily and Emma fulfilled her end of the plan by pinning him down while Colin tossed their remaining snow balls at Will.

"Oh, I see. It's like that, is it?"

The twinkle of mischief in Will's eyes scared Emma and rightly so, because before she knew it, he had her pinned beneath him, packing snow into the hood of her jacket while she squirmed and giggled. Colin clung to his back like a bug, but the little boy was laughing too hard to be of any help to Emma. And truthfully, Emma didn't really mind. She was perfectly happy right where she was—giggling in the park with Will and Colin. Strangely, she couldn't think of anywhere else she'd rather be.

. . .

Will

When they arrived at the skating rink, Will was out of breath from laughter. His cheeks physically hurt from smiling as he watched Emma and Colin trying to make shapes with the steam from their breath in the freezing air. They were walking hand-in-hand like they'd been siblings all their lives and it brought more joy to Will's heart than he'd been expecting.

He tucked his phone away after capturing a few more seconds of video. He'd been sneaking shots all day for another project he was working on. Watching Emma and Colin together made him realize just how lucky he'd been to grow up with his five brothers, and how much he missed them—especially around the holidays. He knew things couldn't stay the same forever, and he was happy his brothers all had exciting lives of their own now, but it still didn't dull the sting he felt of being left behind. And as fun as today had been, Will felt disheartened that his pain had still managed to slip in and steal some of his joy. He wondered if he would ever find a cure for the loneliness that had crept in over the last year.

"What size do you wear?" Emma called, freeing Will from his thoughts.

She was at the skate rental counter, grinning at him. Her hair was a beautiful mess, glistening in spots where little crystals of snow still clung. He hadn't seen her smile like that in a long time, and it pulled him back from the depths of his sorrow. "Thirteen," he replied.

The girl behind the rental counter gave Will a once over. "I like a guy with big feet," she purred.

Emma rolled her eyes. "Keep it in your pants," she muttered.

"I have big feet, too!" Colin yelled standing on his tiptoes trying to look over the counter.

The rental girl gave a humph and handed over the ice skates. Emma paid her and said, "Thanks," with enough frost to resurface the ice rink.

Will took his skates giving Emma a questioning look, which she ignored. The three of them moved over to a bench to lace up their skates. Colin insisted he could lace his own skates, so Will sat down next to Emma and gave her a playful nudge unable to hide his grin.

"What?" she said cooly.

"Keep it in your pants?" Will asked.

Emma rolled her eyes again. "Well, she was being gross."

"My size thirteen feet are gross?"

"Shut up, Will. You know what I mean."

"I don't think I do," he said still grinning.

"Does your ego really need to hear me say that girl was hitting on you?"

He snorted. "And that bothers you?"

"No. It was just inappropriate in front of a little boy."

"I don't think he got the reference, Em."

Emma only looked up from tying her laces to give Will a glare.

He bent down to lace his own skates and leaned into Emma. "I'm a little disappointed."

"Why?"

"I liked the idea that you didn't want her hitting on me."

Emma

Emma stopped mid-lace and looked at Will, their faces mere inches apart as they bent over their skates. This was definitely not her imagination. *Will was flirting with her.* Her heart thumped in her chest. She wanted to reach over and kiss him right now, but she had to be sure this time. She couldn't recover from him making her feel like a complete fool a second time. "Why?" she whispered.

Will smirked. "I've always liked the feisty side of you, Em. But I guess I never pegged you for the girl who defends her guy, and . . . it was nice."

"What was nice?"

"Having you want me." He winked, his vivid blue eyes gleaming with mischief.

"Will . . ." Emma didn't know what to say. Being this close to him was making it impossible to think of anything other than how much she wanted to kiss him. "I . . ." *Was it possible that he didn't know how she felt about him? That he'd never known?*

"It's okay to be jealous, Em."

Emma sat up quickly. "I'm *not* jealous."

"I liked it," Will teased.

Emma huffed, finishing her laces. "Sometimes you're impossible, Will."

He barked a laugh, then moved his lips close enough to brush her ear. "Yeah, but sometimes I'm irresistible," he murmured.

A ripple of desire shuddered through Emma, but before she could react, Will was on his feet and Colin was tugging at Emma's sleeve.

"Come on," Colin whined. "I wanna go skate."

His excited voice brought Emma back to reality. "Do you know how to skate, Colin?"

"Not really."

"Okay, well let's start out slow so you don't get hurt."

"Okay," he said beaming up at her as he slipped his tiny mittened hand into hers.

Will took Colin's other hand and they led him onto the ice.

After a few less than graceful laps around the rink, Colin got the hang of it. Emma was impressed with how quickly he picked it up. But then again, things like ice skating came easier to little kids. She'd always thought that it was the low center of gravity or having a shorter distance to fall. But as she watched Colin skate away, Will trailing him with his phone out to record the moment, she realized it was because kids had no fear. They hadn't been scarred by the world yet. And they hadn't learned that there was so much they could lose if they took a chance and failed.

Emma's eyes found Will. He was skating backward filming Colin, waving and cheering him on. The happiness on Will's face brought such a brightness to Emma's heart that it was almost hard to breathe. She watched them take a lap around the rink, grinning and laughing the whole way. When he came back toward her, Will pulled Emma with him, twirling her once on the ice, until she was clinging to his strong arms to steady herself.

"I've gotcha," he whispered and Emma's heart shuddered with a mix of emotions. *This was the Will she'd fallen in love with. The Will who was always there for her. The Will who made her feel like home.*

They'd spent countless days like this in the park—just being kids and having fun. The small seed of hope Emma clung to grew. She never imagined she'd ever get more moments like these with Will. But somehow he'd made it possible—better even, by including Colin.

The little boy zipped around the skating ring, pushing between them until he held each of their hands again. Emma squeezed Colin's little hand in hers and grinned over his head at Will. His expression seemed to say, '*I told you today would be great*'.

Now if only Emma could tell Will that Colin was only part of the reason she couldn't stop smiling.

25

ill

AFTER SKATING, Will sent a quick text message to signal the next phase of his plan while Emma took Colin to grab some food from the cart vendors. Colin came back with a giant soft pretzel, while Emma held two knishes in her hands. She was practically glowing as she handed one to Will.

"I haven't had a knish in over a year," she remarked. "Do you know they don't sell them in Boston?"

"You're joking?" He had the good manners to look appalled as he shook his head, soaking in her adorableness.

"I tried ordering one at a deli once and they looked at me like I was speaking another language."

"Were you speaking Dothraki?" Colin asked around a mouthful of pretzel.

"No smarty pants, she was speaking New Yorker," Will said ruffling his hair.

Emma bit into her piping hot knish and moaned. The noise was almost obscene and Will struggled to keep his composure as he watched Emma lick the pastry crumbs from her fingers. *He'd never been so jealous of a crumb in his life.*

Luckily, the sound of hooves and bells interrupted his less than PG thoughts about Emma. *Right on time,* Will thought as he turned to see a horse drawn carriage pull up behind them. The driver got out and opened the door, folding out the steps.

"Is that for us?" Colin cried.

Will winked. "You know it, little man."

"This really is the best day ever!" he shrieked.

"Thank Emma," Will said. "This was all her idea."

Colin ran into Emma will all his might and wrapped his arms around her. "You're the best sister in the whole world, Emma."

She knelt down and hugged him back. "You're pretty great too."

"I love you," Colin whispered throwing his arms around her neck.

Will caught the astonished look on Emma's face as she held Colin to her chest. Her eyes glistened with emotion and Will smiled. If he couldn't be with his family, bringing someone else's together was a close second.

He rescued Emma from near tears and hoisted Colin up and into the carriage. Will climbed in himself and extended a hand to Emma. She took it, looking at him with wonder. "Seriously, how did you do all of this?" she whispered.

He shrugged. "I'm full of surprises."

They settled next to each other in the carriage and the driver handed Will a plaid blanket and a thermos of hot cocoa. Colin asked if he could sit up top with the driver, who kindly obliged, which left Will and Emma alone in the back.

This was working out even better than Will had planned. He snuggled closer to Emma in the back seat, stretching the blanket over their laps before pouring her a mug of cocoa as the carriage began its jaunt through the park. The sleigh bells on the horse's harness jingled merrily as they bounced.

Emma grinned. "You really thought of everything, didn't you?" she asked taking the cocoa.

"I don't know about everything."

"Will, I can't thank you enough."

"You don't have to thank me. I just wanted you to have a great day getting to know your little brother."

"Well I did," she said leaning into him. "Today's been perfect."

Will slipped his arm around Emma's shoulder. She fit with him like a missing puzzle piece, so Will wasn't surprised that he felt complete with Emma tucked against him.

"Thank you, Will. It was nice to be a kid at Christmas again."

He smiled. "I still have one more surprise up my sleeve."

Emma

EMMA COULDN'T SUPPRESS her grin when they pulled up to Macy's. The doorman unclipped the red velvet rope to what was dubbed as the *'Path to the North Pole'*. Will led Emma and Colin past festive window displays decked out in holiday cheer and through a winding aisle inside the massive department store until they reached an elevator labeled *'North Pole Express'*.

Colin pressed the button and the doors slid open letting Christmas music spill out. The walls inside of the elevator were wrapped in gold foiled Christmas paper, with red velvet ribbon crisscrossing it to make a perfect bow directly above them. It gave Emma a very Willy Wonka-like feeling of being inside a gift box. As the elevator smoothly climbed to the eighth floor, she glanced up and noticed a bough of mistletoe swaying innocently above her.

"Seriously? More mistletoe?" she asked, looking at Will. *Although she found she didn't mind the insinuating plant as much as she had a few days ago.*

Will shrugged. "It's nearly Christmas. I think our mistletoe moment is unavoidable."

"What's mistletoe?" Colin asked.

Emma laughed. "You speak Dothraki but you don't know what mistletoe is?"

Colin only shook his head.

"Do you wanna take this one?" Emma asked looking at Will.

He grinned. "When you see mistletoe you find someone you like and offer them a high-five. If they high-five you back, that means they like you too."

"Cool!" Colin exclaimed, raising his mittened hand in the air.

Emma tugged Colin's soggy mitten off and high-fived him. Then so did Will. Colin's rosy cheeks glowed. And just when Emma thought he couldn't get any more excited, the elevator doors slid open to the most elaborate Christmas wonderland she'd ever seen.

"Welcome to Santaland," a snow-covered nomad exclaimed. The Nordic actor was brushing the fur of a gigantic animatronic polar bear as fake snow fell over the whimsical scene.

Colin was bouncing on his toes trying to take it all in. There were caroling snowmen, real reindeer and lively elves bustling around carrying stacks of gifts or passing out candy canes to the people waiting in line.

Of course, Will had found a way to make Santaland even more magnificent by securing VIP passes so they didn't have to wait in line to meet Santa. As they walked to the front of the red carpet and Santa came into view, Colin began to shake and

Emma's heart swelled. She remembered what it was like to still believe in that kind of magic and it nearly brought tears to her eyes.

"Is that really Santa?" Colin whispered.

Will knelt down. "Why don't you go talk to him and find out?"

"How will I know?" Colin asked.

"You have to ask for a special Christmas wish and if it comes true you'll know the real Santa got your message."

Colin smiled at Will like he was the most brilliant person in the world, and Emma couldn't help thinking maybe he was.

She turned to Will. "You're going to ask that Santa what Colin wished for, aren't you?"

Will nodded. "I learned a trick or two from my brothers."

"What if he wishes for something you can't get him?"

"He's seven. He'll wish for a new toy or video game."

Emma sighed. "Not all wishes can be purchased. Although, life would be a lot less complicated if they could."

Will looked at Emma with an intensity that made her insides coil feverishly. "Kids don't wish for stuff like that."

"I hope you're right. I want Colin to have a good Christmas. I have a feeling he hasn't had one in a while."

It sounded ridiculous to say after seeing Colin's room. The endless pile of toys and video games showed the boy obviously had more than he needed. But after spending the day with him, Emma could tell the thing Colin really valued was time.

Smart kid, she thought to herself. Emma would do just about anything for more time. More time to appreciate the happy moments she'd had with her parents. More time to figure out where she wanted to go to school next fall. More time to go back and fix her mistakes with Will. *More time to make everything right.*

"Your turn, Emma," Colin said when he bounded back over from Santa.

"Oh, I'm too old to ask Santa for presents."

"You're never to old to make a Christmas wish," Colin argued.

Will chimed in. "Yeah, Em. You're never too old."

"Fine." Emma sighed, feeling ridiculous as she marched up to the Santa performer. He patted his lap and she shook her head. "No way."

"Come on, dear. Don't be shy."

Emma looked back at the line of people waiting. This was absurd. There were little kids dying to get their turn with Santa. She didn't want to make them wait. The best thing to do was just get this over with quickly. She balanced herself on the Santa impersonator's knee.

"So, tell me . . ." Santa began.

"Emma."

"Ah yes, Emma. What's your Christmas wish, Emma?"

She resisted the urge to roll her eyes. "I wish . . . I wish . . ." But the words stuck in her mouth. Emma stared back at Will and suddenly all she wanted was another chance with him. "I wish I could make things right with him," she whispered.

"That's a tall order, young lady."

"What?" Emma looked at the Santa in shock. She hadn't realized she'd even said anything out loud.

"If you open your heart, maybe your wish will come true."

Emma stood abruptly. Suddenly she wanted to be anywhere but there. "Thanks," she mumbled hurrying off the stage.

"Did you make your wish?" Colin asked when she rejoined him and Will.

"Yeah," she muttered, still feeling a bit shell-shocked.

"You're next, Will," Colin instructed.

Will gave them a wink and jogged over to Santa. Emma watched as he leaned in to whisper something in Santa's ear. Santa laughed and whispered back, wiping the confident smirk from Will's face. He glanced back at Emma and Colin and frowned. Emma watched as Will reconfirmed whatever the Santa-clad man had told him. But Santa only shook his head. Will thanked him, shook his hand and walked back over to Emma and Colin, wearing the same dazed expression Emma had when she'd left the stage.

26

ill

THE RIDE DOWN in the elevator was much less euphoric than the ride up. They were in a different car and it wasn't decorated as festively as the one that took them to Santaland. The mistletoe was notably absent. And after what the Santa impersonator told Will, he wasn't sure if that was a good thing or not.

Will kept glancing at Emma cautiously. It's not that he didn't believe Santa, or Franklin, rather. Franklin was the son of the super in Will's building. He was only a few years older than Will, and was going to school for acting in the city. He'd been moonlighting as Santa at Macy's for the past few years. So when Will was planning his day with Emma and Colin, he'd asked Franklin to tell him what they wished for so Will could swoop in and be the Christmas hero.

Of course Will hadn't taken into account that both Emma and Colin would wish for things that he couldn't buy. Will had been completely caught off guard by both of their requests. Colin wished for 'the best Christmas ever.' A nearly impossible task considering Will didn't know anything about Colin's previous holidays. And with Emma's wish . . . he didn't even know where to start. She wished she could make things right with him. *Had she meant Will or Colin? And if she had meant Will, what had she done that she needed to make right? Did it mean she wanted something more?*

Will was still pondering the endless possibilities of meanings when they arrived at the ground floor. The elevator doors slid open and they filed out, starting toward the exit until Colin pulled them back.

"Wait," Colin called tugging at Emma's arm.

"What's up?" she asked.

"Will you help me pick out a Christmas present?"

She smiled. "Sure. Who's it for?"

Colin waved her closer and whispered something in her ear.

Emma stood up and looked slyly at Will. "Oh, okay. Sure. That's a good idea, buddy." She faced Will. "Do you mind if we do some quick shopping?"

"Yeah. Of course." Will started to follow them back into the maze of fragrances and cosmetics but Emma held her hand up.

"You kinda need to sit this one out," she whispered nodding toward Colin, who was grinning like a criminal.

"We're picking out something for you," Colin said shyly.

Emma put her hands on her hips. "Colin, it's not a surprise if you give it away," she teased.

Colin giggled. "Oops!"

Will laughed and took the pile of jackets from Emma's arms. "I'll wait at the café on two. Have fun."

"Thanks." Emma grinned and took Colin's hand.

As Will watched them go a knot tightened in his stomach. He needed to find a way to save their Christmas, and quickly.

. . .

Emma

"I'M TELLING YOU, he'll love it," Emma said reassuring Colin for the hundredth time that Will would like the tripod they'd picked out.

"But I don't even know what it is?" Colin complained.

"That's because you're not a film maker. But Will is and he's going to love your gift."

As soon as Emma had seen the mini flexible tripod she knew it was the perfect gift for Will. He had a few larger ones he used with his professional cameras but this one would fit in his pocket for easy access when he was filming with his iPhone like he had been today.

Colin sighed, still unconvinced. "Maybe you should give him the Gorillapod and I should give him the tie."

Emma laughed. There was no way she was giving up the tie. She found an identical one to replace the one Will had used as a tourniquet on her leg. "The tie is sort of an inside joke for us."

"Why?"

"I kinda ruined one of his ties at a party the other night."

"The night you stayed at Will's house?"

Emma stopped walking. "How did you know I stayed there?"

"Will texted Dad to tell him you were sleeping at his house. I heard him and Mom fighting about it."

Emma cringed for many reasons. It still felt weird to hear Colin call her father, Dad. But also, she couldn't believe Will had been thoughtful enough to let her father know she was safe. Or that her father had a reaction at all. *Had he been worried about her?*

"Did my dad sound angry?" Emma asked.

"Oh yeah. But Mom told him to give you some space."

That was even more shocking. If anything Tara should've been ratting Emma out for her snotty behavior. *What was Tara's angle?*

"Is Will your boyfriend?" Colin asked interrupting Emma's thoughts.

Emma flinched at the word. "No."

"Why not?"

"It's complicated."

"But you like him?"

She nodded, unbelievably flustered to be admitting that to a seven-year-old when she hadn't even fully admitted it to herself.

"And Will likes you," Colin said like it was plainly obvious.

"Why do you think he likes me?" Emma asked.

"He's nice to you."

"Will's nice to everyone," she said. *Almost to a fault.*

"Yeah, but he asks Dad about you all the time."

Emma felt her heart flutter. "He does?"

Colin grinned. "I think he *loves* you."

"Colin!" Emma hissed. "You can't go around saying things like that."

"Why not?"

"Because . . ." *What could she say? Because she didn't know how she felt about him? Because if he did, she wasn't sure she knew what that would mean?* Colin looked expectantly at her. "Can you just trust me on this one?"

Colin chewed his lip as if he was truly mulling it over. He finally sighed. "Okay, but I still don't think we found Will the perfect gift. He's the coolest and I want to get him something great."

"Tell you what," Emma said. "We'll give him the Gorillapod first and if he doesn't like it, I'll say it's from me and you can give him the tie."

Colin scrunched up his face. He wasn't buying.

"And Christmas is still a few days away, so we'll keep searching for the perfect gift."

"Deal!" Colin said, sticking his hand out.

Emma shook it. "You drive a hard bargain, little man."

Colin looked delighted with himself.

"I had fun with you today," Emma admitted.

"Me too. It was the best day of my life."

Emma's heart melted a little more. She glanced at her phone to avoid looking at Colin's adoring face for fear she might cry. But when she saw the time she frowned. They'd been gone longer than she planned. "We better get home. Plus, Will's been waiting."

Colin held Emma's hand on the escalator, cheerfully chatting as they made their way to the Herald Square Café on the second floor. Emma saw Will sitting at one of the high-backed bar chairs with his back to them. Their jackets were piled on the empty chair next to him, but Emma's eyes went directly to the occupied chair across from Will. Liz sat there, twirling a piece of her long black hair around her finger, grinning like Christmas had come early.

Emma's heart plummeted. *What the hell was Liz doing here?* Emma watched in horror as Liz snapped selfie after selfie of her and Will, leaning in disgustingly close. *God, she was like a freaking stalker-azzi!* But then Emma reminder herself that for all she knew, Will had called Liz. He could deny that they were a couple all he wanted, but there was definitely something going on between them. Emma knew the Manhattan social circle was small. But casual acquaintances didn't run into each other that often. And there was nothing casual about the way Liz was running her hands over Will's shoulders. It looked more like she was staking her claim.

Emma considered sneaking away, but Colin blew that plan out of the water when he marched through the busy café calling to Will, holding his giftwrapped present in the air.

Liz sneered when she saw Emma scuttling up behind Colin. "Emmy! What a nice surprise. And who is this?" Liz asked looking at Colin.

"This is Colin Emerson," Will said making the introductions. "Colin, this is Liz Vanderveer."

"Hi Liz. You're pretty."

Liz practically purred. "Oh aren't you precious? You're Tara's son, aren't you?"

"Yep. And Emma's brother," Colin replied proudly.

"Is that so?" Liz asked smugly.

"Hey look!" Colin exclaimed pointing to the ceiling. "Mistletoe."

He held his little hand up to Liz for a high-five, but she didn't see it, considering she was busy crushing her painted red lips against Will's.

Emma pounced, tackling Liz from her chair and beating the conniving wench with her velvet Gucci stilettos. *At least that's what she did in her head.* In reality, Emma only lunged for Colin's hand. She gave him a swift high-five and gathered their jackets before dragging him abruptly from the café.

"Wait? Why are we leaving?" Colin protested. "What about Will?"

"Will's busy."

"But—"

"No buts, Colin. We need to go!"

Colin pouted but he didn't protest as Emma tugged him to the elevators, even as they heard Will shouting after them.

27

Emma

EMMA HELD it together until she got Colin buckled into the cab she hailed outside of Macy's. But as they pulled away, the silence gave her too much time to think. All the images of Will and Liz over the years began to overwhelm Emma. *Who was she kidding?* She couldn't compete with Liz Vanderveer. She'd never be like her and she didn't want to be. But the thing that made her heart ache the most was the thought that if Liz was the kind of girl that Will liked then there was no hope for Emma.

She looked out the window, biting her lip to keep her tears at bay. *How was she still so stupid?* She had let a few good moments with Will give her hope. The searing pain that clenched her heart alerted Emma to the fact that she hadn't realized her foolish heart had been knitting itself back together over the past few days. But it was evident now as she felt it tear apart all over again. *Had she learned nothing from her parents' divorce? Letting people in only allowed them to hurt you.*

"I'm sorry you're sad," Colin said.

Emma swallowed back the tightness in her throat. She didn't trust her voice so she only nodded.

"Why did Will kiss that girl?"

Emma shook her head. "That's a good question." *And one Emma might never have an answer for.*

Will

WILL TAPPED his foot in frustration as his driver maneuvered the limo back toward his building through rush hour traffic. He'd tried Emma's phone a dozen times with no answer. His chest coiled tighter as he flashed back to the image of Emma climbing into a cab and speeding away from him. She'd glanced back only once and the hurt he saw in her eyes stopped Will in his tracks. He couldn't get that image out of his mind and it gutted him to think he had caused Emma that kind of pain.

They'd been having such a perfect day, but of course Liz found a way to screw things up as usual. She'd texted Will saying she had a message from his parents, and when he mentioned he was at Macy's Liz appeared out of thin air, claiming she'd been getting a manicure next door.

And not only did Liz show up to hijack his date with Emma, she also dropped the bombshell that Will would be on his own for Christmas. Apparently they'd called Tom to tell him and Hazel they were extending their trip and asked them to get a message to Will. They hadn't even had the decency to call him. He was crushed. And of course Liz took the opportunity to console him. Will shouldn't have let her, but his mind was reeling. He had barely heard the soothing words or comforting touches Liz offered through the sickening disappointment that coursed through him. But Colin's voice had jerked Will out of his spiral of despair, just long enough for Liz to take advantage of the mistletoe strung above their heads. *Will was really starting to hate the meddling plant.*

The kiss meant nothing to Will. But it couldn't have happened at a worse time. He'd seen the hurt flair in Emma's stunned eyes. And by the time Will got Liz to retract her claws, Emma was already gone.

IT SEEMED to take forever to get back to his building. And as Will took the elevator to his floor, he scowled at the mischievous plant swaying above his head. He reached up and ripped it down, but it didn't make him feel any better. Will couldn't blame all of his troubles on a plant. If he wanted things to change it was time he went after what he wanted—starting with Emma.

Will steeled himself as he knocked on Emma's door. It was time he ended this game and told her how he felt. She answered looking puffy-eyed which only knotted Will's stomach more. She'd changed into pajama pants and an oversized sweater. Her blonde hair was pulled up in a messy bun. He'd seen Emma this way a million times before—all casual and warm, but he'd never wanted to pull her into his arms and kiss her so badly before. His heart ached with longing.

"Can we talk?" Will asked.

Emma didn't reply. She simply stepped into the hall, pulling the door shut quietly behind her.

Will could tell from her body language that she wasn't in

the mood for small talk. Her arms were crossed tightly across her chest and she chewed her bottom lip—something she only did when she was trying to hold back saying things she shouldn't.

"You can say it," he offered softly.

"Say what?"

"That I'm an idiot."

She huffed. "Well at least you know it."

"I'm sorry about today."

"What part?" she asked. "That Liz showed up, or that you got caught?"

"Em, no! It's not like that." But her scowl cut him off. Will raked his fingers through his hair in frustration. "I don't know how else to tell you there's nothing going on between me and Liz."

"You can say it all you want, but Snapchat says otherwise."

"Excuse me?"

Emma groaned, rolling her eyes. "Why do you have to be the only person in Manhattan not on social media?"

"Because none of that shit matters. It's not even real life. It's a bunch of desperate people showing you what they want you to believe so you'll like them more. It's mob mentality and it's everything that's wrong with our society."

"I'm not debating the importance of social media with you right now, Will."

"Fine. But if we're getting into it, why don't you tell me what happened the night of the winter formal? Or why you left without saying goodbye? I thought we were friends, Emma. I thought we were more than that, but you just cut me out of your life like I was nothing. Do you have any idea how much that hurt?"

"Good. I'm glad it hurt. I hope it hurt as much as you making a fool out of me."

He blanched. "How did I make a fool out of you? You're the one who stood me up in front of the whole school!"

"You looked just fine to me," Emma sneered.

"Wait. Were you there?"

"I didn't have to be there, Will. I saw the pictures online."

"What pictures?"

"Really? Are you going to deny dancing with Liz all night?"

"No but—"

Emma snorted. "You really did look perfect together. How am I supposed to compete with that?"

"Emma, I'm trying to tell you that you don't have to compete. I wanted *you* there by my side. I've always wanted you."

"Yeah," she scoffed. "You looked really broken up about me not showing. I mean especially in the after party pics from Cranston's."

Will looked down shamefully. "I'm not gonna deny that I got drunk, Emma. But . . ."

"But what? It was my fault?"

"No! But you made me feel like shit. Like no one cared about me at all. My parents have never really cared and I can deal with that. I expect that. But you . . . I thought you'd always be there for me. But you turned into a ghost for no reason."

"Oh, there was a reason."

"Then tell me what the hell it is so I can fix it!" he shouted.

"Why don't you ask Liz?"

"I did! She doesn't know what you're talking about."

Emma scoffed. "Of course she'd say that."

Will wanted to scream. "This conversation is going nowhere."

"Then why are we having it?"

"Because we should've had it a year ago!" he bellowed throwing his hands up. "Because I still care about you. I never stopped. And I need . . . I need you to know that I miss you." He moved closer, tugging Emma's hand free so he could hold it. "Being with you these past few days has been amazing." He moved closer, daring to let his fingers sweep away a stray lock of her hair. "I don't want to lose you again," he whispered pulling her into his arms.

Emma pulled away. "Will, I can't do this."

"Em, please just let me say this, because I've meant to for a long time. I care about you. And I know you care about me too. I can feel it when we're together. I want this," he said picking up her hand again. "I want us."

Hurt swam in her eyes. "There *is* no us, Will."

"Why not?"

"I don't even live here anymore."

"You could move back. I mean you're coming back for college, right?"

"No. I thought maybe, but . . ." Emma shook her head sadly. "You should just leave me alone, Will. It's better off that way."

"No it's not," he argued, unable to keep the anguish from his voice. "You know it's not, Emma. New York will always be your home. This is where you belong. . . with me."

Emma closed her brilliant green eyes and released a tight breath trying to compose herself.

Will ran his hands up her arms holding her in place. "Emma, I want you. I've always wanted you. Just tell me you feel the same and I'll do whatever you want," he begged.

When she opened her eyes he barely recognized her. "What I want, is for you to leave me alone. I'm going back to Boston in a few days, and I want to pretend this holiday never happened."

"How can you say that?" Will demanded, but he could see Emma was shutting down, putting up the wall she never let anyone behind—*anyone but him.*

Emma already had one hand on the door to her father's apartment. "I leave the day after Christmas," she said calmly. "I need to spend time with my family."

"And what am I supposed to do?" he asked.

She shrugged. "The same."

"That's kinda hard when my family isn't coming home."

Emma's eyes flickered up to his with concern. *A chink in her armor.* "They called?" she asked.

"No," he laughed gruffly. "They sent Liz. That's what she was doing at Macy's today. Telling me my parents don't care enough to come home for Christmas, in case you wanted to know the real reason we were talking instead of getting your gossip from Snapchat."

But there it was again, the simmering anger at the mere mention of Liz's name. Emma's hand twisted the doorknob and Will swallowed his pain. He was done. Done pouring his heart out only to get it stomped on. His parents didn't care. Emma didn't care. *What the hell was the point of holding onto hope for those who only trafficked in disappointment?*

Will didn't want to feel like this anymore. Maybe Emma had the right idea—build up your defense and ward off the pain before it could find a way in.

Deflated, Will sighed. "Have a good Christmas, Emma." Then he turned back toward his apartment and walked away.

Emma

EMMA MADE it to the bathroom before she burst into tears. She turned on the shower to drown out her sobs as she slid to the floor and dissolved into a full-blown ugly cry. *What the hell was wrong with her?* Will had just told her he wanted her. He'd said everything she could've hoped for. *So why wasn't it enough? Why did she still feel so heartbroken?*

Because there's no going back, the little voice in her head told her. *Because he betrayed you and broke your heart the day he went into that closet with Liz and nothing will ever make it go away.*

No matter what sweet things Will said or did, he couldn't take it back. He had broken the magic they'd spent a lifetime building for a few hormone and booze fueled moments with Liz. *Maybe more than a few.*

But it didn't matter. Liz had punched Will's V-card and that meant he'd compare everyone to her for the rest of his life. Emma couldn't deal with that. She could barely stand competing for popularity with Liz in the halls of St. James. She damn sure wasn't going to compete with her between the sheets. Especially not when Liz bragged about all the hours she clocked on her back.

He made a mistake, Emma's conscience chided. Everyone's entitled to a bad choice here and there. But bad choices were acid wash jeans, not bedding Liz Vanderveer in Cranston's closet after he'd asked Emma to the formal. Emma choked on her tears as her emotions warred against each other. She wasn't perfect. She knew people made mistakes and she wasn't above forgiving them. But this felt like a stain on her soul that only a miracle or a time machine could erase.

EMMA MANAGED to pull herself together long enough to shower and get ready for bed even though it was barely seven o'clock. She'd told Tara she wasn't hungry when she'd knocked on the bathroom door saying she was ordering in for dinner for Colin, so Emma was surprised to find a large brown takeout bag on the kitchen counter with her name on it. There was a note next to it.

Emma, I'm meeting Teddy for dinner. Colin already ate and is in bed. He had a wonderful time with you today. Thank you for taking him out. I wanted to make sure you had dinner tonight, but I don't know what you like, so I ordered a little of everything. Enjoy. – Tara

EMMA PEERED inside to see half the menu from Café China inside. Grateful, she pulled out a few of the square white boxes and dished the piping hot rice noodles, sesame chicken and stir-fried vegetables onto a plate before smothering it with coconut curry sauce.

She sat down on the couch and devoured her meal, not realizing how hungry she'd been. She was emotionally drained and somehow the food filled her with a tiny bit of comfort. After cleaning up the kitchen, Emma settled in on her makeshift couch bed and told Penelope to play a Christmas movie. She flipped threw a few before settling on '*Elf*.' It always made her laugh and she could use as much happiness as she could get at the moment.

It seemed Colin was a fan of the movie too, because he came running out of his bedroom when he recognized the soundtrack. He paused when he saw Emma, making Hodor crash into the back of him.

"Hi, Emma," Colin said brightly. "Are you watching Elf?"

"Yep."

His little cheeks curled into perfect pink circles as he grinned. "That's my favorite Christmas movie."

"It's a good one," Emma replied. "Do you want to watch it with me?"

"Can I?" he asked sounding surprised.

"Sure," she said pulling her knees to her chest to make room for him on the couch.

Colin didn't hesitate a moment. He bounded onto the

couch, calling Hodor up too. Colin looked up at Emma like he just realized maybe she would be mad about the dog on the furniture. "Sometimes I let Hodor on the couch when Mom and Dad aren't here," he whispered. "Don't tell, okay?"

Emma couldn't help herself, she smirked at his serious tone, nodding that she would keep his secret.

The three of them settled in to watch the movie. Halfway through, Colin snuggled up next to Emma. His eyes were drowsy and kept blinking closed.

"Do you want to go to bed?" she asked.

"No. I'm not tired," he said stifling a yawn. "I want to hang out with you."

Emma smiled and pulled the blanket up over Colin's little shoulders, making Hodor groan and flop onto his side. She shook her head at the lazy dog taking up half the couch, but she couldn't deny he was a good foot warmer as she wiggled her toes further under his glossy coat.

"Emma?" Colin murmured.

"Huh?"

"Are you still mad at Will?"

Emma's heart tightened. *Will.* For about five minutes she'd managed not to think about him. But hearing Colin mention his name was like an icicle to the chest.

"I'm not mad anymore," she said. "Just sad."

"I don't want you to be sad."

"Me either," Emma admitted.

"When I'm sad, I let Hodor sleep with me. He always makes me feel better."

Emma looked at the drowsy dog sprawled across her feet. He did have a calming presence. Colin looked at the dog too, chewing his lip like he was deciding something. Then he turned to Emma. "If you want . . . Hodor can sleep with you."

There was so much hope in Colin's voice that Emma's throat was suddenly tight. She pulled the little boy closer, hugging him tight as tears pricked the corners of her eyes. *How had she almost missed bonding with this kid?* He was sort of awesome, and the sad part was, Emma had Will to thank for their new found friendship.

She was a mess of emotions as she whispered. "Thanks, buddy. That's really nice of you."

"You're welcome," Colin murmured, his voice sleepy again.

28

ill

WILL SPENT HALF the night at the gym punishing himself on the treadmill and in the weight room after his conversation with Emma. If nothing else, at least his lacrosse coach wouldn't be able to ride his ass for slacking over the holidays. Ever since Emma showed up in New York, Will had been hitting the gym extra hard. It was his only outlet for his pent up frustrations over her. *The girl was driving him insane and she had no idea.*

Emma was a total smoke show. She'd always been. And maybe it was because he hadn't seen her in a while or because he knew she was sleeping just down the hall from him, but Will hadn't had a good night's rest since she arrived. And when he did manage to sleep, Emma haunted his dreams, filling them with tantalizing illusions of kissing her perfect lips or tracing her rose petal skin.

Just that morning Will had woken from a dream so real he

swore his skin felt scorched from Emma's touch. He'd had to start the day with a cold shower. Will could hardly believe it was still the same day. *How had things gone so wrong?*

He'd planned the perfect date for he and Emma to help her get to know Colin, all the while showing her everything there was to love about New York, and about him. Will had been sure if he could help her remember how great things used to be when they were together they could get back there—to that place they were when everything was perfect. When they were Emma and Will. When he never could've imagined her not in his life. He just wanted to go back to how things were before she left. But Emma had made it clear that wasn't going to happen. Will upped the speed on his treadmill, trying to outrun the reality of Emma's harsh words, but in the end he walked home feeling broken and alone.

AFTER EXERCISING his demons at the gym, Will chucked his gym bag in his bedroom and took his second cold shower of the day, wondering how things had gone from a dream to a nightmare in the span of a few hours. He was still way too wound up to go to bed despite it being nearly midnight, so he turned to his first love—the classics. But even Will's old black and white films couldn't bring him any comfort. They only reminded him that he used to watch them with Emma and it made him miss her more.

It was infuriating knowing she was next door and there was nothing he could do about it. It was taking all his willpower not to march to her apartment and drag her back into the hall to finish their conversation, because it wasn't over. *It couldn't be over.*

Will wanted to fight for her. And he'd seen that spark in her eyes when they'd been in the park. His mind flashed back to their perfect day. Her laughter ringing out as he chased her with snowballs. How she'd held onto him on the ice. The warmth of her next to him in the carriage. The way their eyes met across the room. He hadn't imagined it. And if only to prove it to himself, Will switched off '*Casablanca*' and flipped opened his laptop. He'd uploaded the videos he'd stealthily taken throughout the day.

Proofing the clips, Will paused at certain intervals to memorize the stolen moments between him and Emma. They were there. Every last one of them. And that only made him even more upset. *How could she feel the way he did and not want to fight for it?*

So what if she lived in Boston and he was in New York? They were only a few hours apart. And in a few short months they'd be graduating and could go anywhere. There were great film schools in Boston. And there wasn't anywhere better for fashion than New York. They could make it work.

Will had always thought that Emma would come back to the city for college. That had been her plan since she went to her first Fashion Week in fifth grade. She'd come back and told him she wanted to go to Parsons and open up her own design studio in the garment district. And Will was perfectly happy with that plan because he planned to stay in the city too and go to Columbia. He didn't have a choice since his parents and brothers were all distinguished alumni. But Columbia had a great film program and all that mattered was that he and Emma would be together.

His chest felt tight as he realized a major flaw in his plan. Will had mapped out his entire future without ever telling Emma the most important part. That he wanted her in it. That *she* was his future—the axis around which his universe rotated. *God, how had he let that happen?*

He suddenly felt ridiculous for having been too afraid of losing her to admit that he was in love with her. Because he absolutely was. And look where trying to deny it had gotten him. He'd kept his stupid mouth shut and lost her anyway. And right now nothing was more terrifying.

"I'm not giving up," Will muttered to himself. It wasn't over yet. He had to believe he still had a chance. He may not agree with his parents' choices most of the time, but he had learned one thing from them. *Go after what you want one hundred percent or not at all.* Emma was what Will wanted. And he wouldn't quit until she believed him.

29

ill

WILL RUBBED his eyes and looked at the clock again. It couldn't be eight in the morning already. He hadn't even slept. But then again, he knew sleep wasn't an option. Not with so much on the line. He ejected the jump drive and shut his laptop, praying what he'd done would be enough. He wrote Emma's name on a small cream envelope and slipped the tiny jump drive inside. He added the note he'd written, sealing it with a prayer that he could get through to her.

Emma

EMMA STIRRED SLOWLY, the watery morning light spilling into the living room. She heard a faint snoring and bit her lip to keep from laughing when she located the source. Hodor was sprawled across her legs snoring contently, while Colin was curled up half on top of the dog and half in Emma's lap. She tried to move her legs but they were asleep. When she finally managed to dislodge one, Hodor's chocolaty eyes snapped open and his tail began to thump against the couch.

"Mom?" Colin murmured groggily.

"It's just me, buddy. Go back to sleep," she whispered slipping out from beneath him.

He happily obliged as she covered him back up with the warm blanket. Hodor gladly nestled on top of it, too. Emma scratched his soft head affectionately. Colin was right—the dog really did make her feel better. And she'd slept great considering she'd been sharing a couch that looked more like an art exhibit than furniture with a seven-year-old and a giant dog.

Fighting the pins and needles in her legs, Emma padded barefoot across the cold white marble floor to the guest bathroom. She sighed gratefully when she noticed someone had turned on the heated floors in there. She washed her face and brushed her teeth, frowning as she examined the pale purple shadows beneath her eyes. The stress of the past few days had definitely taken its toll. She swept her hair up into a messy bun and applied her favorite pale lip gloss and mascara, pinching her cheeks to get a little color in them. She forced a smile at her barely improved reflection. "Good enough," she muttered.

Emma didn't know why she was bothering. It's not like she had anyone to impress. There were only two days until Christmas; three until she returned to Boston. She hadn't seen her father since she arrived, and Tara was scarcely around . . . not that Emma was eager to spend time with her mother's replacement. But besides Colin, Emma could go the rest of her time in New York without seeing another friendly face. Will was definitely excluded from that category after last night.

Just the thought of him sent a spike of pain through her

chest. *God, why couldn't she just get over him?* She'd thought she'd moved on until she came back to New York. *Would it always be like this? Would she stare longingly down the hall to his apartment wondering what might have been every time she came to visit her father?* That is, *if* she came to visit her father at all after this trip. So far her father had done a pretty good job at showing Emma having her in his life wasn't a priority.

She sighed trying to push her depressing thoughts away. She was over feeling sorry for herself. She still had a few days left in the city and she was determined to make the most of them. She'd made a mental list of all the things she missed about New York on the train ride from Boston. The food, the fashion, her friends. *Okay so maybe friends were off the table . . .* But that didn't mean she couldn't still take in the sights and savor some of her favorite cuisine. Besides, she still had to make her decision on where she wanted to go to college. So far, Boston was the clear front runner. But Emma was having a hard time letting go of New York.

There was a knock on the bathroom door and Emma cracked it open to see Colin grinning at her. He thrust an envelope into her hand. "You got a present," he sang in an excited voice.

Emma took one look at her name printed neatly across the cream paper and knew instantly it was from Will.

"Open it, open it!" Colin demanded.

Emma did, letting the jump drive slide into her hand. She looked inside and pulled out the note.

Emma, your future is here. You belong in New York. You belong with me. Just give me one more chance to prove it. – Will

"What is it?" Colin asked bouncing on his toes.

Emma looked at him. "Where did you get this?"

"The front door."

"Colin, didn't we talk about not opening the door to strangers?"

"It wasn't a stranger. It was no one. There was a knock but no one was there. Who's it from?" he asked pointing to the note.

"Will," Emma said quietly.

A worried expression flickered across Colin's face. "But it's not Christmas. We don't have the perfect gift for Will yet!"

"I'm not sure this is a gift," Emma replied studying the tiny jump drive. A miniature label stuck to it, and written in Will's perfect penmanship was a message. *I hear there's some really great fashion schools in New York.*

"Then what is it?" Colin asked.

Emma's nerves snapped like live wires in her veins. The stubborn streak in her made her want to march down the hall and leave the jump drive at Will's door, unopened. It was the only chance she had of possibly moving on without him. But she knew there was no way in hell that would happen. Her curiosity was already piqued.

She pushed passed Colin, padding to her pile of things in the hall. She dug out her laptop, frowning when it showed the dead battery symbol instead of her home screen. *Not again!* She desperately needed a new laptop. The damn thing was barely holding a charge lately. But that was the least of her worries at the moment.

She turned to Colin. "Do you have a computer I can use?"

"Sure!"

Emma followed Colin into his room and sat in his desk chair while he flipped open a laptop. She handed Colin the jump drive and watched as he expertly inserted it and opened the file before climbing onto her lap. As she's expected, it was a movie file. Will used to make Emma all sorts of funny little films when they were younger. They were the only gifts they'd ever exchanged, actually. There was a time when Emma loved to play the actress in Will's films. Her favorite part had always been pulling together an elaborate wardrobe from her closet, prompting Will to tell her she should be a Hollywood costume designer.

The memory stung, but not so much as what Emma saw when the film began. A black screen flashed ten words. *'I hear there are some great fashion schools in New York.'* The next screen had two simple sentences. *'New York, meet Emma Rhodes. Your next design star.'*

What followed took her breath away. It was image after image of her. Emma in the park, twirling in the first skirt she ever made. Emma running up and down the isles of Mood Fabric. Emma grinning as she bent bright-eyed over her sewing machine. Emma modeling her fashion finds from Brooklyn's vintage clothing stores. Emma pretending to catwalk down the hallway at St. James, rocking her unique style in her altered school uniform. It went on and on.

Will had hundreds of clips of Emma. Some she'd forgotten about, and some she had no idea he'd even filmed. As she watched her fashion montage, her heart hemorrhaged with emotion. Emma barely recognized the girl Will had captured on film. *When was the last time she'd smiled like that?*

Fashion had always made Emma happy. She'd known it was her passion since the very first runway show her mother had taken her to. But lately Emma hadn't felt inspired enough to devote much time to her passion. She felt lost, just trying to hang on to the frayed pieces of her old life.

Moving to Boston and starting at a new school hadn't been easy on her. And even after she'd settled into her new life, things still hadn't clicked. It was like a phantom piece was always missing. And until that very moment Emma hadn't realized what it was. But now she did. She'd left her passion in New

York. It was like the city itself somehow inspired her to create. And without it, she'd lost a part of who she was.

Emma hadn't realized how much not having that spark to create had affected her. It had stolen away part of her heart, where creativity and inspiration lie. And Will had known it. He'd taken one look at her and known what was missing. That was how well he knew her. He knew what Emma needed even when she didn't. Her heart thumped like a jackhammer in her chest. *She'd made a huge mistake.* Will was right—she belonged in New York. She belonged with him.

Now if only Emma could figure out how to get past the memory that sliced her heart to pieces every time she thought of moving forward with Will. *Why? Why did it have to be Liz Vanderveer that he took into that closet?* Anyone else Emma was sure she could get past. But Liz was practically Emma's nemesis. And she would always be a part of Will's life.

Emma bit her lip as she watched the final clips of the video. It faded to black and another sentence appeared on the screen. '*Emma Rhodes. The future is yours.*'

Tears spilled down her cheeks and she hadn't realized how tightly she was holding Colin in her lap until he tried to wriggle out of her arms to look at her. Emma quickly swiped her tears away.

"That was *so* cool! Did Will really make that movie?"

She nodded.

"And you made all those cool costumes?"

She nodded, laughing at Colin referring to her designs as costumes. But in a way they were. They were like fashionable armor that gave her the confidence and ability to believe she could do anything. *And maybe she still could.*

An idea glimmered in her mind for a moment and she put Colin down so she could focus on it. She paced his room for a minute before turning to him with a smile. "I think I have a plan for Will's perfect gift."

Colin bounced on his feet. “What is it?”

“Get dressed,” she said. “And wear something warm.”

“Where are we going?” Colin called after her as she left his room.

“To a Christmas tree farm.”

30

ill

WILL SHOVED past Sharon when he heard the knock at the front door. “I got it,” he called, prompting an exaggerated eyebrow raise from the sassy housekeeper.

When Will opened the door to find Emma standing there his heart nearly stopped. He felt his face light up with hope and relief. “Does this mean you’re giving me another chance?” he asked.

Emma bit her lip as a soft smile made an appearance. “Maybe.”

“Then what are you doing here?” he asked.

Will had been hoping his film would show Emma how much he cared and that he’d never stopped caring or planning for their future together. His stomach had been in knots since he left the envelope at her door. He’d assumed the radio silence had meant one thing—his plan hadn’t worked. But here was

Emma, standing at his door, dressed like she was planning a winter expedition.

"You helped me find something I'd lost. I want to do the same for you."

"How?" he asked, still confused.

Just then Colin came thundering down the hall dressed in boots, a winter jacket, hat, scarf and gloves. "I'm ready!" he yelled sprinting toward them.

Will turned back to Emma who was grinning. "By keeping your Christmas tradition alive," she said, with a twinkle in her eyes as she held up a set of keys.

"WHY DO I FEEL LIKE A FUGITIVE?" Will asked after hoisting Colin into the cab of the old beat up pickup truck.

They'd taken Will's car service to a parking garage outside the city where Emma's father kept his cars. But Will hadn't been expecting the set of keys Emma held to belong to the antique Ford rust bucket.

"Because you're a Manhattan brat and haven't ever ridden in a car that wasn't a limo," Emma teased.

"Hey! I've been in Cranston's Ferrari."

Emma gave him a trying look.

"Right, not helping," Will said. "But seriously, whose truck is this?" he asked staring at the massive steering wheel.

"It's my mom's!" Colin perked up. "And her name is Jezebel."

Emma and Will both raised their eyebrows at that.

"And does Jezebel still run?" Will asked.

"Like a champ, according to Tara," Emma offered.

Will gave the dusty dash a pat and held his breath as he turned the key in the ignition. He expected the truck was more likely to explode than start, but surprisingly it roared to life with authority.

"Well, that's a good sign. Maybe this crazy plan will actually work," he joked.

"Have a little faith," Emma ordered. "Besides, how else are we supposed to get the perfect Christmas tree home from your magic tree farm that's a million miles outside the city?"

Will looked at her like she was crazy. "They have a delivery service, Em."

"Oh." The flustered look on her face was so adorable that Will could barely contain his amusement. "But, we're here," he said. "Might as well have an adventure."

"Yeah!" Colin exclaimed from his spot on the patchwork bench seat between them.

Will grinned. "Buckle up."

Emma

EMMA WAS certain she'd never live her pickup truck blunder down when they'd pulled out of the garage and the old truck backfired loud enough to cause people on the street to stop and stare. Some even dropped to the ground, probably thinking it was gunfire. Colin thought it was awesome, of course. And Will's echoing laughter almost made up for Emma's embarrassment. She'd been beyond grateful when Tara offered up the use of her truck to help Emma and Colin pull off Will's Christmas surprise, but Emma was beginning to wonder if maybe Tara was finally paying her back for her more than frosty behavior over the past few days.

Luckily, the rest of the road trip was going much smoother. An hour outside the city, Will stopped for gas at a station that looked like an old barn.

"We always stop here for syrup on the way," he explained.

"Syrup?" Emma asked, quirking an eyebrow.

Will winked. "You'll see."

Colin ran down the aisle loading up on road trip snacks, which turned out to be Slim Jims, M&Ms and Mountain Dew. Will grabbed coffee for himself and Emma, and a large mason jar of local maple syrup, grinning wider than Colin.

"Want anything else?" Will asked before paying the guy at the counter.

Emma grabbed a pack of wintermint Tic Tacs and added them to their loot on the counter.

"I should've guessed," Will added with a smirk.

"What?"

"You're obsessed with those things."

"Am not."

"Oh please," Will teased. "When we were thirteen you told me you'd rather give up TV than Tic Tacs."

Emma's heart hiccupped. "Do you remember everything about me?" she asked guiltily.

"Of course," Will answered looking at her like she'd asked something everyone already knew the answer to.

Emma followed him and Colin out to the truck in a bit of a daze. It had begun to snow and she watched Will lift Colin under the arms and twirl him around through the snowflakes before safely depositing him in the truck. Colin's laughter pealed through the crisp December air and something in Emma's chest cracked open. She felt as though she was looking at Will for the first time. He was still the same old Will—the boy who'd been her kind, dependable best friend. But now, as she took him in, the fine shadow of stubble shading his jaw, the slight curl to his dark locks that peeked out from under his navy beanie, the comfortable fit of his gray pants and work boots . . . all she saw was her future.

She'd never seen this version of Will—so comfortable in his

own skin. So happy and alive. And suddenly she ached to be the one twirling in his arms under the soundless fall of snowflakes. She wanted to kiss his frost-bright cheeks, share the curling frozen breath between them.

He turned to look at her as if he knew what she was thinking. "What?"

She shook her head, feeling her cheeks glow. *How had she ever thought she'd get over this boy?* This morning she'd been sure she could. But then Will's video had changed everything. And when she embarked on this Christmas tree adventure she'd told herself it was just as friends. But clearly it was much more than that.

Emma approached the truck but stopped as she noticed Will rubbing the back of his neck in thought as he stared at the gas pumps.

"What's wrong?" she asked.

"This is kinda embarrassing, but I don't know how to pump gas."

Emma burst out laughing. "Move over, Miss Daisy" she said playfully shoving him aside.

"Have I ever told you how good you are for a guy's confidence, Em?" Will remarked.

Emma rolled her eyes. "Okay are you ready for your first gas pumping lesson, city boy?"

"Hey, you're just as much a city brat as I am."

"Yeah, but now I'm a Boston city brat. And in Boston, we pump our own gas."

Will smirked and gave a mock bow, allowing Emma to proceed with the gas. Will blew into his ungloved hands to keep them warm as they waited for the massive tank to fill. "So," he murmured between puffs of steam. "What changed your mind?"

"About what?" Emma asked.

"Me."

"Who says I've changed my mind?"

"You're here. I just figured it meant something."

Emma sighed deeply and a cloud of swirling air hung between them. "I didn't want you to lose your holiday tradition." She stuffed her free hand in her pocket. "It seems like we've both already lost enough."

"Have I lost you?" Will asked quietly.

When Emma met his gaze, she felt scorched by the intensity in Will's exquisite blue eyes. "I don't know," she whispered.

"Em—"

"Will, I don't think we can go back. Too much has happened."

"Then maybe we can go forward?"

Emma looked at him, wanting more than anything to say yes. She wanted to trust him, but it was hard. But maybe, just maybe they could carve out a new path. It was Christmas after all, with a new year just around the corner. *What better time to forge a new beginning?*

"I think I'd like that," she said, but as Will's face filled with delight she added, "But as friends first."

"As friends first," he clarified, his grin dazzling her.

His joy was contagious and she couldn't hide her smile as she agreed. "Deal."

31

Emma

EMMERICH TREE FARM was everything Will had said and more. Emma felt like she was inside a Christmas greeting card as they boarded the horse drawn wagon that took them out to endless fields of pine trees. Will helped her and Colin down once they reached the Douglas fir section, which according to Will, was the only acceptable kind of Christmas tree. He handed Emma the leather gloves and a large red hacksaw they'd borrowed from the tree lodge, before lifting Colin onto his shoulders.

Colin was in his glory scouting for trees from atop Will's broad back. Emma snapped pictures of them as she walked behind, taking in the blissful holiday haven. She never expected to enjoy being lost in the winter wilderness as much as she was. For as much as she teased Will, Emma was a city brat through-and-through. *Or at least she thought she was.* But as

Emma glanced at Will, drinking in his gorgeous features, she wondered if she knew herself at all.

"We found it!" Colin shouted, pulling Emma back to reality. "We found the perfect tree!"

Will let Colin down from his shoulders and the little boy raced ahead to find the tree he'd spotted, while Will waited for Emma to catch up. He took the saw from her and slung an arm around her shoulders.

"So what do ya think?" he asked gesturing to the massive expanse of the farm.

"You were right. It's magical here."

"I always wanted to bring you here," he added.

"Really?"

"Yeah."

"Why didn't you?"

"I was sorta saving it for when . . ." he trailed off, cheeks reddening.

"For when?" Emma asked.

"I don't know if I should say."

"Why?"

"We're barely in the friends zone, Em. I don't want to freak you out."

"Oh come on. You can't say something like that and then not tell me. I promise I won't freak out," she said. "I swear on my sewing machine."

"Whoa! The sewing machine. That's serious."

"I know. Now tell me."

Will rubbed the back of his neck again. A sure sign he was nervous. *Oh God, what was he saving this place for?* The troves of teen horror movies Will had dragged her to flashed in her mind, and suddenly Emma wasn't so sure she wanted to know.

"I was saving it for when we had our own family to bring out here."

Emma stopped walking. Her whole body was seized with a tingling shiver. "What?"

Will turned to face her. "You promised you wouldn't freak out."

"I'm not," she said her eyes wide with panic.

"Uh, you sorta look like you're freaking out. Could you maybe blink or something so I know you're not having a stroke?"

Emma blinked rapidly and looked up at Will's worried expression. "You think about stuff like that?"

"Yeah. All the time." He flushed, rubbing his neck again. "Or at least I used to."

Never had Emma wanted to leap into his arms more. She wanted to kiss Will and melt into this moment where they could stay frozen for all of time. Because his simple statement had been a wrecking ball to the crumbling wall she'd been trying to build around her tattered heart. And in that moment, she saw a life with Will flash before her and she wanted it more than anything.

Neither of them had the families they wanted, but together, they could start their own and the idea was equal parts terrifying and euphoric.

"Em?" Will moved closer, his hand going to Emma's cheek. "Take a breath."

She did.

"Let's go get a Christmas tree. We can talk about this later if you want."

She nodded and took the hand he offered, trying to ignore the tightness in her throat.

Will

. . .

WILL DID his best to push his stupid blundering moment of honesty to the back of his mind, but it was nearly impossible. Especially when he kept catching Emma looking at him like that. Like he was someone she knew but couldn't quiet place. *Why the hell had he chosen now to admit that to her?*

He was seriously hopeless at being friends with Emma. But he'd rather be in her life as a friend than not at all, no matter how painful it was. He'd let his guard down completely the day they took Colin to Central Park. And when the three of them had ice skated hand-in-hand he knew that was it. There was no other alternative for his future. Will wanted Emma in it or no one at all.

Will didn't realize until now how scary that was to admit to himself. Or how quickly his heart could be torn to bits if Emma decided she didn't want him. But still, he couldn't stop trying. He was so close. He could feel it in the space between them. It was like the electric charge in the air right before a lightning strike. Emma was on the edge of a cliff and he just needed to convince her to fall—to convince her she was safe, because he would always be there to catch her.

It was a blessing that the tasks ahead of them were so labor intensive. Cutting down the tree and dragging it back to the wagon would serve as a great distraction. And then there was Colin. His glee did wonders to lighten the mood.

Will let Colin and Emma take turns using the saw on the towering Douglas fir they'd chosen to take home. And when the tree was ready to fall, he even let the little boy give it the final kick that sent it crashing to the ground.

"Timber!" Colin called jumping up and down.

Roughly an hour later, they arrived back at the lodge with their prize tree between them in the horse drawn wagon. Will returned the saw and gloves while the staff prepared the tree, wrapping it before loading it in the back of Jezebel.

"That was so much fun!" Colin exclaimed. "Your tree is so much better than ours."

Emma laughed. "I can't disagree with you there, buddy."

"What's wrong with your tree?" Will asked.

"What's not?" Colin remarked. "It's fake, white and small."

Will laughed. "That *is* bad."

"I wish we could get a real tree for our house," Colin whined.

"Maybe next year," Emma replied.

"You guys hungry?" Will asked changing the subject.

"Starving," Colin replied.

"Good. They have the best burgers in New York here. And save room for dessert. I'm gonna run out to the truck and grab the maple syrup."

"Ah the mystery maple syrup is finally making an appearance," Emma teased.

Will winked. "I'll meet you inside. Grab a seat by the fireplace if you can."

While Emma and Colin headed inside the lodge, Will ran over to the guys wrapping his tree and slipped them a few extra bills to throw in a tiny tree for Colin and Emma's apartment too. He smiled as he jogged to the truck, wondering if maybe he'd actually pull off a Christmas miracle after all.

32

Emma

EMMA COULDN'T STOP GIGGLING as she watched Will pour an unhealthy amount of maple syrup over his snow cone, which according to the waitress, was made with the snow right outside the lodge.

After the waitress left them, Will and Colin started an outbreak of yellow snow jokes that made Emma's sides hurt. They'd wolfed down their burgers in record time and moved to the comfy couches near the roaring fireplace where their snow cones were served.

"You laugh but once you try it you'll be hooked for life," Will teased.

"Oh you think?" Emma remarked

Will gave her a cocky smirk. "I dare say you'll like it better than your precious Tic Tacs."

Emma sucked in a dramatic breath and put her hand to her chest. "Never."

Will looked conspiratorially at Colin. "She's a Tic Tac junkie, that one."

"Hey, I may be a Tic Tac fiend but at least I can pump my own gas."

Colin collapsed into a fit of giggles and pointed at Will. "Emma wins!"

Will frowned. "Fine, but just for that, I'm not sharing my syrup."

"Too late," Colin called swiping the syrup off the table and dousing his snow cone. He passed it to Emma, who did the same and then took a bite of the frosty treat.

"Omigod," Emma groaned. "You weren't kidding."

The warm syrup melted chunks of the snow into crunch candy crystals that melted in her mouth like the finest sugar.

Will gave Emma a Cheshire grin when she devoured her cone and asked the waitress for another. He added a round of homemade apple cider to the order and Emma thought she'd died and gone to heaven when she took her first sip of the hot cider dolloped with whipped cream and a cinnamon stick.

"Will, this place is heavenly," she murmured between sips as she curled her hand around the warm mug.

"I'm glad you like it," he said hitting her with a smoldering gaze.

Emma felt her stomach flip. *Damn. When had Will learned to dial his smile up to heart failure level?*

"I want to live here!" Colin added.

"Me too, buddy," Will replied. But he checked his watch quickly. "Unfortunately we better be getting on the road. We've gotta get Jezebel home before the roads get icy."

~

Even the ride home was magical. Colin sat between Emma and Will and had quickly fallen asleep thanks to the loud rumble of the engine and the warmth of the truck cab. His little head slumped against Emma's side, prompting her to scoot closer so she could tuck him under her arm.

Will took the close proximity as an opportunity to stretch his arm across the back of the bench seat, and then Emma's shoulders. He was presently tracing lazy patterns on her arm that made her pulse quicken.

"Thanks for doing this, Em."

"Doing what?"

"Making today happen. I really needed it."

"You're welcome. Besides, it was fun."

"Really? Even with everything I blurted out?"

She smiled shyly, not quite able to meet his glance. "Even with that."

Emma could see Will's wide smile ripple into place from the corner of her eye. She loved when he smiled fully like that. It was so rare and boyish and it suddenly made her toes curl.

"Do you want to talk about it?" he asked.

"I think that conversation might be better when it's just the two of us," she replied.

"I don't know. Colin sorta makes for a good buffer. I know you won't get mad at me in front of him."

Emma looked at Will, startled. "I wasn't mad, Will. Just surprised."

"Good surprised?" he asked hopefully.

"I don't know yet," Emma replied. "But I'm glad you told me. And I'm really glad I got to go the tree farm with you. I see why you love it so much."

"Yeah, it's a pretty amazing place. But it's always been more about the people I share it with than the farm itself."

Emma nodded, knowing what he meant. She understood why the tradition had been so special to Will. She'd glimpsed slivers of it today—what it would be like to share season after season there, watching love and family grow with the height of the trees.

"Do you think . . . maybe you'd want to go back there with me? Next year?" Will asked.

A powerful feeling gripped her heart, screaming the answers to the questions she was terrified to ask. *Yes! This is what you want Emma! Will is who you want! Tell him yes! Yes to New York. Yes to him. Yes to everything.*

"I think I would," she whispered.

Will grinned. "I can work with that."

Will

AFTER PASSING off the old pickup truck to the stunned car service in front of his apartment building, Will took Colin from Emma's arms. The little boy was still fast asleep. Will cradled Colin to his chest as the doorman opened the door and called an elevator for them.

"Thanks, Winston," Will nodded. "And tell Devon and Pete there's a few extra Franklins for all of you for your trouble with the trees."

"No trouble at all, sir," Winston replied.

The elevator doors slid closed and Will and Emma were shrouded in silence. He glanced over at her and she was smirking at him.

"What?" he asked coyly.

"Nothing."

"Don't say nothing. I know that look, Emma Rhodes. You're thinking something devious."

"No I'm not."

"You like what you see, don't ya," he joked. But to his surprise Emma shrugged.

"Maybe I do."

Pride and hope erupted in his chest, and the combination left him overly confident. He nodded to the resilient mistletoe someone had rehung in the elevator. "If you like what you see so much . . ."

"Oh, do you want another high-five?" Emma taunted.

"My hands are a little full," Will retorted.

The elevator doors dinged, sliding open to their floor.

"Hmm. That's too bad," Emma said stepping off the elevator and stunned him with a smile. "I was feeling caught up in the holiday spirit for a moment."

Will nearly tripped over himself following her out of the elevator. *She was gonna be the death of him.* He loved flirting with Emma, but it had always been one sided—until now. With her flirting back his heart didn't stand a chance.

33

Emma

WILL HELPED Emma get Colin tucked into bed before leaving to help the building staff with his tree. Emma used the extra time to freshen up. She didn't know what had come over her, but something had changed during the drive home. Something that made her brave enough to want Will. Or at least brave enough to entertain the possibility of it.

She brushed out her long blonde hair and changed into her pajamas, cursing herself for not packing anything cute. All she had was the same red plaid bottoms and a deep blue long sleeve top that had the words, *'J'adore Dior'* printed in gold foil letters. She slipped on a pair of fuzzy argyle socks and headed for the door, stopping to pop a Tic Tac for good luck.

By the time Emma got to Will's, he already had his massive tree in the tree stand thanks to the burly hotel staff that was just leaving.

"Wow, cutting it a little close?" Emma asked pointing to the top of the tree that was dangerously close to the ceiling.

"Nah, it's perfect," Will replied. "You look comfy," he noted, taking in her appearance.

"Oh, yeah." Emma nervously looked down at her unflattering pajamas. "I needed to get out of my boots, so I went for comfort."

"Good call. Give me a minute to change," Will called disappearing down the hall. "You can start on the lights if you want."

Emma stared at the four plastic containers labeled '*Taylor Christmas.*' *Was that an invitation to stay and decorate?* She'd only planned to come over to thank Will for another great day and perhaps kiss him goodnight if she didn't lose her nerve.

But when Will jogged back out looking positively delicious in his own plaid pajama bottoms, fuzzy socks and gray t-shirt she decided she would definitely stay if he offered. He still had his beanie on and when her eyes flicked to it he seemed to remember and pulled it off, sending his dark locks into chaos. He ran a hand through his hair but it only made it worse.

"Here," Emma offered reaching up to smooth down his snow-damp hair. The sensation of it slipping through her fingers did unmentionable things to her insides. "There," she said pulling her fingers away before she got carried away.

"Thanks," Will replied, his voice thicker than usual.

They both stood there staring at each other for a long moment before Will cleared his throat. "I'm gonna grab some of Sharon's famous eggnog. Do you want some?"

"Sure," Emma whispered, second-guessing her bravery.

THE EGGNOG DEFINITELY HELPED. Three glasses later Emma couldn't remember why she'd been so nervous to be alone with Will. Christmas music blared, a fire roared and Will's tree was perfectly decorated. The only thing left to do was adorn the top with the star. But the two of them couldn't agree on the best method.

"I could Elf it," Will suggested.

"Elf it?"

"Ya know, get a running start and jump off the couch."

Emma snorted. "Because that turned out so well for Elf."

"Okay, what's your idea, genius?"

"Put me on your shoulders."

Will scratched his chin. "That could work, but . . ."

"But nothing. It'll totally work."

"I don't know. You're kinda like the eighth dwarf . . . tipsy."

Will laughed at his joke and Emma scowled at him. "I am not. I haven't even had anything to drink."

Will smirked at her. "You know there's bourbon in the eggnog, right?"

"I do now!"

He laughed. "Maybe maintenance can bring up a ladder."

"You can't call them at midnight and ask for a ladder," Emma scoffed. "Just man up and put me on your shoulders."

"Okay but if this goes down like a bad cheer stunt remember you suggested it."

"Will Taylor, did you just make a cheerleading joke? Have you been watching '*Bring It On*' without me?" she teased, referring to the summer she'd wanted to try out for the cheerleading team and made Will watch all the '*Bring It On*' movies on repeat only to chicken out at the audition.

"Just get over here already," he said sounding exasperated.

Will knelt down so Emma could sling her legs over his shoulders.

"You ready?" he asked.

"Ready."

"You better use those spirit fingers to hang on tight," he instructed before standing to his full height.

Emma shrieked, wrapping her hands around his face, only to feel him shaking with laughter. "What's so funny?"

"You never would've made the cheerleading squad."

"What? Why not?"

"You're sorta choking me out with your thighs. And it would be helpful if you didn't hang onto my face. Being able to see is kinda crucial."

"Oh, right," Emma said laughing. "Sorry." She slid her trembling hands to his head instead, but she still couldn't quite command her thighs to unclench. "Is that better?"

He laughed, handing her the star. "It'll do."

Will moved closer to the tree and Emma strained to lean far enough to place the star on top. Once she got it into position she slowly removed her shaking hands. When it stayed she let out a *whoop* and clapped her hands. "We did it!"

"Now for the dismount," Will announced.

"What?"

But Emma's answer came when Will shifted suddenly to the left and her world tilted violently. She shrieked closing her eyes, sure she was about to end up headfirst of the floor, but an instant later she felt Will's strong arms around her, cradling her from the fall.

"I've got you, Em," he whispered, his voice warm against her ear.

She opened her eyes and stared into his. Will was smiling at her in a way that would ignite a Yule log. "You know I'd never let you fall, right?"

She nodded silently, still gazing into the sparking pools of his blue eyes. *God, she wanted to drown in them.* But she was frozen, powerless to turn this magic moment into something more. And just like that it passed.

Will set Emma on her feet and backed away to take in the Christmas tree in all its splendor. "That's a damn fine tree," he announced.

Emma moved to his side to admire it and agreed. "It's perfect."

"Sorta makes ya wish Christmas came more than once a year, right?" Will added.

Emma snorted. "I don't know if I could handle that."

Will gave her a troubled look and pulled her over to the couch. Emma knew that look. It was his problem-solving look.

When they were sitting, much closer than necessary, Will took her hands. "So you made my Christmas suck a little less," he murmured. "Tell me how I can fix yours."

"I'm not sure that's possible."

"Oh come on. Is it really that bad?" he teased. "You might not be Teddy and Tara's biggest fan but at least you're not gonna be alone for Christmas."

Emma stared at Will for a quiet moment before she did what she'd come over here to do. "Neither are you."

"Did you get me tickets to Dubai? Because I'm certain there's no way my parents are cutting their trip short anytime soon."

"No."

"Then I'm still gonna be alone for Christmas."

"No you're not," Emma said surer this time. "Spend Christmas with me."

"Really?" he asked sounding surprised. "That's what you want?"

"Yeah, we're friends, right?

"Right," he whispered, looking at her in that way again. That way that made her hot and bothered in all the right places.

"But don't get your hopes up," she warned. "Christmas at my father's probably won't be any better than being here alone considering he hasn't included me in any of his plans since he got here, but . . . there's no reason we should both be alone on Christmas."

Will squeezed Emma's hands for a quiet moment, then looked into her eyes. "Emma thank you for including me. I'll be there. But can you do one thing for me?"

"What?"

"Talk to your father. Tell him how you feel or things are never gonna change."

Emma rolled her eyes. "Sure, I'll talk to him when you talk to your parents."

"I tell my parents how I feel all the time. I don't matter enough to them, but you matter to your father."

Emma's heart broke a little to hear Will say he didn't matter to his parents with such acceptance. "What makes you think my father's any different than your parents?"

"Because he was a good father to you before the divorce. And I know he still cares about you. We talk about you all the time. I think he just doesn't know how to be a part of your life anymore. You chose your mother over him and he's not sure how he fits anymore."

"He said that?"

Will nodded.

"Why would he ever think that?" But as soon as the words were out of her mouth, she knew exactly why. Up until the pictures from Cranston's and the winter formal started circulating, Emma had decided to stay in New York with her father. But the next day, heartbreak and embarrassment had driven Emma to take her mother's offer to move to Boston and escape her problems. Emma packed her things and left with her mother right before Christmas without even offering anyone an explanation, including her father.

"I know how he feels, Em. It hurts to be left behind. It makes you feel like you're not good enough."

"I never wanted anyone to feel like that," she whispered. "It's just . . . I was a mess. I'm still a mess."

"Then talk to him. Tell him that. Don't leave things unsaid. Especially not with the people you love."

Will was staring at Emma so intently she knew they were no longer talking only about her father. There were many things left unsaid between Emma and Will too. And as they inched closer to each other on the couch, the things Emma longed to say came dangerously close to spilling out.

But today had been perfect. She didn't want to ruin it. Or rather let Liz ruin it by bringing her back into the conversation. Emma closed her eyes and pushed Liz Vanderveer out of her mind.

"Maybe now is a good time to continue our conversation from the tree farm," she ventured.

Will looked down for a beat, seeming to collect himself. "I'm sorry I blurted it out like that, Emma. But it's how I feel. It's how I've always felt."

"So you want to have a family with me?"

"I want everything with you, Em."

"Don't you think we're skipping a few steps?" she asked.

"Maybe. But I don't want to lose you again. I don't think I could survive it."

Emma closed her eyes again. Guilt lanced her now that she knew how badly she'd hurt Will. She'd never meant to. When she opened her eyes Will was only a breath away. He stroked her cheek before tucking a strand of hair behind her ear. His fingers lingered softly at her jaw, tilting it ever so slightly toward his.

Emma's breath hitched, her face so close to Will's that his breath brushed her lips teasingly. Her whole body tingled with anticipation as Will trailed a finger down the column of her neck. It felt like tiny flames were licking a trail beneath his touch. Emma sighed and leaned into him.

"God, I want to kiss you," he whispered.

"What's stopping you?"

"You are."

Emma's glassy eyes blinked open. "What do you mean?"

"Do you want me to kiss you, Emma?"

"I think so," she said breathlessly.

"When you know without a doubt . . . I'll be waiting."

Then, before Emma knew what was happening, Will stood up and led her to the door.

Befuddled, Emma found herself alone in the harsh light of her building's hallway, with an ache deep in her bones.

Will

REGRET FLOODED WILL the instant he shut the door. His libido chastised him as every last ounce of blood in his veins screamed at him to rush into that hallway and pin Emma against the wall until he kissed her like he'd always wanted to —like his life depended on it. Because at the moment it felt like it did. He felt like he might have lost his damn mind letting her walk away when she'd been willing to let him kiss her.

Let, he reminded himself. He didn't want to just have Emma *let* him kiss her. He wanted her to want it, to need it, the way he did. The way he felt it deep in his bones.

Will ran his hands through his hair in frustration, muttering obscenities as he marched to his bathroom, cranking the shower knob as cold as it would go.

Emma

EMMA STUMBLED into her father's apartment, still confused as to what went wrong with Will. But her confusion only grew when she heard her father call her name from somewhere in the dining room.

She paused, thinking she must truly have lost her mind. *Since when did her father wait up for her?*

She popped her head in just to make sure she wasn't hallucinating. But there was her father, clutching a glass of scotch with a tired expression etched into the lines of his face. Emma blinked hard. *How much eggnog had she drank?*

She felt like she was visiting the ghost of Christmas past—where her father still drank scotch and Will was oblivious to Emma's advances. If her mother came waltzing down the hall next, Emma was going to run screaming from the the house.

"Where have you been, Emma?" her father asked sounding more upset than he had any right to.

"At Will's," she said defensively.

"Oh." He looked as though her answer had taken the fight out of him. "You could at least let us know where you are."

"Since when do you care?" she spat.

He father stood so abruptly the chair screeched backward and Emma retreated a step. Seeing her do so must've dissolved her father's anger. His face crumbled as he sat back down, taking a long drink from his glass. "I guess I deserve that."

"I'm sorry, Dad, but you kinda do."

"Do you want to talk about it?" he asked.

"Not really," she muttered, turning to leave even though her anger was simmering.

"Fine," he replied shaking his head. "But I'm disappointed in you."

Emma whirled around. "Me? What about you?" Emma screeched.

She marched back into the dining room and laid into her father, unleashing all her frustrations thanks to the liquid courage provided by the eggnog she'd been knocking back at Will's.

She'd thought after what Will had told her, she'd go easy on her father, but something had snapped inside her tonight when Will sent her home wanting. Emma was through being denied the things she wanted in life. And she wanted a relationship with her father. She wouldn't settle for being shoved aside and she was going to make sure he knew that.

When she was done, her chest was heaving and she'd spewed all her injustices. The fact that she didn't have a bedroom, the way her father had unloaded Tara, Colin, a wedding and a pregnancy on her without any warning, and how he hadn't made any time for her since she'd come home. But when Emma looked at her father, who'd stayed uncharacteristically quiet through her rant, he was grinning, which only fueled her irritation. "Why are you smiling?"

"Because I'd take you yelling at me any day over ignoring me. If you're yelling it means you still care. At least it did with your mother. That's how I knew it was over between us, your mother and me, I mean."

"Oh," Emma said sinking down into a chair at the table.

Her father smiled wistfully. "You're so much like her, ya know?"

Emma nodded. She was the spitting image of her mother, right down to the blonde hair, green eyes, and apparently, fiery temper.

Her father reached across the table and took Emma's hand. "I want to make sure you understand something, sweetheart. When things fell apart between your mother and I, I wasn't at my best and I'm sorry for what that did to our relationship. But I want you to know no matter what happens, nothing will ever make you stop being my daughter. I love you so much, Em. You know that, right?"

Emma's eyes welled as she looked at him. She'd wanted to hear him say that for so long. Her throat bobbed as she swallowed back her tears and nodded. "I know, Dad."

"And you're right. I need to do a better job of showing you that. This apartment was only meant to be temporary. It's part of the reason I didn't want you to come to the city yet."

"What do you mean?"

Her father sighed. "I was hoping to keep this for part of your Christmas surprise, but the reason I haven't been around very much is because I've been meeting with a team of builders who are working around the clock to get our new home ready. I was hoping it would be finished by Christmas, but they're behind schedule. It'll be New Year's Eve at best."

"You're moving again?"

He nodded. "We all are."

"Do I have a room there?"

He nodded again, grinning this time. "Would you like to see it?"

"Yes," Emma said breathlessly as warmth and love bloomed in her chest. *He hadn't forgotten about her after all.*

"I can't wait to show it to you. It's really something. You have a great big bedroom and attached . . . well, I'll let that be the surprise. We can go tomorrow morning if you'd like, just me and you."

"I'd like that, Dad."

"Good. Just don't tell Tara and Colin yet. I want it to be a surprise."

"I won't."

Her father stood and walked over to her chair, pulling it out so he could wrap her up in a hug. "Emma, thank you for talking to me. I love you, sweetheart."

"I love you too, Daddy."

34

ill

THE NEXT MORNING Will stumbled out of bed. It was Christmas Eve and his level of regret had reached an all time high. *What the hell had he been thinking last night?* He still couldn't quite believe he'd sent Emma home without kissing her. He knew it was the right thing to do, but sometimes he really wished he wasn't the guy who always did the right thing. *Where had it gotten him?*

Alone on Christmas, that's where. *Well maybe not totally alone.* Emma had invited him to spend Christmas with her family last night. But then again, that was before Will stupidly shut her down and sent her home when she was finally looking at him the way he'd always wished she would.

After a quick breakfast, Will dressed and decided to go knock on Emma's door. It was the only way he'd get rid of the nagging feeling in his gut that he'd royally screwed up. Plus, he didn't much feel like spending another minute alone in his apartment. It felt emptier than usual since he'd already sent the entire staff home to enjoy the holiday with their families. They at least deserved to be with family and loved ones even if Will couldn't.

Sharon had been the hardest to convince, but he persuaded her after saying he'd be spending Christmas with Emma. Sharon was practically gushing as she served him breakfast and showed him where all the meals she'd prepared were. After a few more minutes of motherly fussing, she seemed satisfied that he would manage without her for a few days and headed out the door wishing him luck.

Will checked his reflection in the foyer mirror before stepping out into the hall. *Was it ridiculous that he was this nervous to knock on Emma's door?* He suddenly wished he had one of her silly Tic Tacs. *Get a grip, Will. She's not gonna open the door and kiss you.*

Will shook his head at himself. *He seriously had to stop watching so many girly movies with Sharon.* He mustered his courage and marched down the hall, knocking loudly on the door before he lost his nerve. It opened a moment later and Will was met with Colin's glowing smile. "Hi, Will!"

"Hey, Colin. Is Emma here?"

He shook his little head and pouted. "She's gone."

Will's stomach dropped twenty stories to the lobby. "Gone? Where did she go?"

Colin's pout deepened. "She wouldn't say."

Shit! Why the hell didn't he just kiss her last night? What if shutting her down had sent her running again? *Christ! It was last year's winter formal all over again.*

"Colin," a cheerful voice called from inside the apartment. "What did I say about answering the door for strangers?"

"It's not a stranger, Mom. It's just Will."

Tara appeared behind Colin. She was a sight in a red dress with a plunging neckline. “Will, honey, how are you?”

“Hi, Miss Emerson. I’m well. And you?”

“Please call me Tara, honey. And we’re fabulous,” she said patting her baby bump. “How can I help you?”

“Oh, I was just stopping by to speak to Emma but it appears I missed her.”

Tara grinned. “Oh yes, she and Teddy left early this morning. Something about a Christmas surprise? They were both being quite mysterious. It was adorable.”

Will’s heart leapt. “So she’s not gone?”

“I should hope not. She told me she’d watch Colin while Teddy and I attend the Christmas Eve garden party tonight.”

“Oh, that’s great. Thank you, Miss Emerson, I mean, Tara.”

Will was already hurrying down the hall when Tara called after him. “I’ll tell her you stopped by.”

“Thank you!” Will jogged down the hall, his heart thumping wildly in his chest. It wasn’t over yet. He still had a chance. *And he might even have a plan.*

Emma

“Dad!” Emma gasped when they walked into the new penthouse apartment on Fifth Avenue. “It’s phenomenal.”

The place was massive and nearly finished. It seemed the kitchen was the last piece of the puzzle. The dazzling marble counter tops and rich cabinets were installed, but there were wires and pipes sticking out where the appliances and sinks should be. As they walked further into the massive luxury suite, Emma noticed things were further along. She recognized pieces of furniture and art under layers of clear plastic and her heart leapt. They were from her old home. *Her father hadn't gotten rid of them after all.*

Emma turned and threw her arms around his neck.

Her father's stern face creased with a rare smile. "I take it you approve?"

"It reminds me of home," she said beaming at him.

"That's what I was hoping you'd say. Come on, I can't wait till you see your room," he said leading the way.

Emma followed her father into a massive bedroom with an en suite bathroom and walk-in closet the size of her whole bedroom in Boston. Her old canopy bed and dresser were already set up inside. "This is for me?" she asked in awe.

"Yep. It's all yours," her father answered. "And this," he said opening a door to an adjoining room, "is your studio."

Emma's mouth fell open as she stared into the room. She felt like she was staring into a dream. There were mannequin forms, sewing machines, bolts of muslin and fabric, and an entire glittering wall of accessories. And on a drawing table in the corner, was a brand new MacBook Pro adorned with a red bow.

Emma couldn't hold her tears back. Her trembling hand flew to her heart as she took in the designer's paradise. "Dad . . . how did you know?"

"You're my daughter, Emma. How could I not know?"

Emma ran into her father's arms and sobbed into his chest. She let him stroke her hair until she could compose herself. When she stopped shaking, her father put his steady hands firmly on her shoulders.

"Emma, ever since we bought you your first sewing machine, you wanted to be a designer. I know a lot has changed since then, but not everything. I still know my daughter."

She nodded bleary-eyed.

"I also know you have some big decisions regarding college next fall. And I'm not going to try to influence that decision. But if you want to choose a school in New York I want you to know we'd be thrilled to have you."

Emma grinned through a hiccup. "And this isn't supposed to influence my decision?" she asked sarcastically as she gazed at the design studio.

Her father chuckled. "You can't blame a father for wanting to give his daughter the best, can you?"

Emma laughed. "I guess not."

"I love you, Emma. And whether you choose a school here or half way around the world, that's not going to change, okay?"

"Thanks, Dad. I love you too. And this means so much to me."

Her father frowned. "Why do I sense a *but* coming?"

"It's just, I don't need all of this."

"What *do* you need, sweetheart?"

Emma stared into her father's warm blue eyes. They reminded her of Will's and she felt a knife twist in her heart. She threw her arms around her father again to stave off the pain. "I just need you, Dad."

"Oh sweetie, you have no idea how good it is to hear you say that."

Emma pulled back. "Dad, I need to tell you something?"

"Anything, sweetheart."

"It's sort of a long story. Maybe I can tell you over breakfast?"

"How does Jean-Georges sound?"

Emma grinned. "Perfect."

35

Emma

AFTER A SPECTACULAR BRUNCH AT JEAN-GEORGES, Emma couldn't put off her conversation with her father any longer. The problem was, she didn't know how to start. *How could she tell her father the real reason she left was because a boy broke her heart?* Especially if she didn't want him to kill said boy.

"So any chance you'd like to start this long story of yours?" her father asked glancing at his watch.

"Is there somewhere you have to be?" she asked. "I don't want to hold you up. We can talk later."

"Oh no you don't. I have all the time in the world for you."

Emma sighed. "Okay, but can you promise me you'll remain impartial about some of the characters in this story?"

He raised his eyebrows. "I can promise you I'll try."

"So last year, when I left New York with Mom, it wasn't because I was choosing her over you."

"It wasn't?"

Emma shook her head. "It was because of a boy."

"A boy?"

Emma could already see her father's stern features hardening. "Dad, I can't tell you this if you're going to get all Tony Soprano on me."

That made him chuckle. "I'll do my best."

"Okay, so this boy, who will remain nameless for now, I'd kind of had a crush on him forever, but I didn't think he ever really thought of me that way, until last year when he finally asked me out. I was so excited." Emma felt her heart squeeze at the memory. "But before we could go out I found out he hooked up with another girl at a party."

"How did you find out?"

"Some friends sent me pictures of it. And at first I didn't want to believe it. But the next day I saw them together at school and I just knew it was true. I was so embarrassed and heartbroken. I didn't know what to do. And then Mom asked me one more time if I wanted to come to Boston and suddenly it seemed like the only way out. So I took it."

"And what about now?" her father asked.

"What do you mean?"

"I assume you're telling me this because something has changed?"

Emma shrugged. "I don't know. I mean in some ways nothing has changed. I've always loved the city. And being back here reminds me how much I miss it. And how much I miss you."

"And what about this boy?"

"I still love him, Dad. But I don't know if I can trust him. But the thought of not at least trying to make it work . . ." Emma's face folded in despair.

Her father took her hand. "Sweetheart, I'm going to try to give you advice as someone who's had their fair share of tumultuous relationships. Love isn't easy. But it's always worth it."

"But how do I know it'll work out?"

"You don't. But that's just the chance you have to take. If your heart is showing you a path toward love, you owe it to yourself to follow it through."

Emma bit her lip and looked at him.

"Emma, there's not much certain in life. But love, no matter how long or fleeting, is always worth it."

"How do you know when it's real?"

He thought for a moment. "I suppose you don't, because you never truly know how someone else feels. But you have to be able to trust yourself and your heart."

"Is that what happened with you and Mom?"

Her father looked sad for a moment before answering. "Your mother and I hadn't loved each other for a long time. And when I met Tara, it reminded me of that." He sighed. "I know I didn't set a good example for you with the way things happened between your mother and I. But don't let our mistakes scare you away from making your own."

"But I don't want to make mistakes, Dad."

He smiled. "Sweetheart, we all make mistakes. Sometimes it's the only way we learn what we want out of life."

Emma thought about that for a long moment. *Had Liz been Will's mistake? Could Emma forgive him for it? Or would trusting him be her big mistake?*

"Em, I've made my fair share of mistakes when it comes to relationships, but I wouldn't change anything about my life. Your mother and I did love each other for a while. And when it fell apart, it was one of the hardest things I've ever been through. But I survived. And I'd go through it all over again if I had to, because without it I wouldn't have you in my life." He smiled warmly at Emma. "And now I've found love again."

"With Tara?"

He nodded. "I know others judge the way Tara and I got together, but I wouldn't change that either. If we waited for the timing to be right maybe it never would have happened and that would be a shame, because that woman is a blessing in my life. She makes me happy and she's brought Colin and soon, a new baby into our lives. I really want you to get to know her, Em. She has a good heart."

"I think I'd like that, Dad. I'm sorry I didn't give her a chance before. I just felt like you were choosing her over me."

"It's not a competition, sweetheart."

"I know that now. But Dad . . ." Emma chose her words carefully. "What about Mom?"

"What about her?"

"I don't want to be the one to tell her you're getting married to Tara and having another baby."

Her father smiled, shaking his head. "Your mother already knows everything, Emma. I asked her to give me time to tell you."

"You did?"

"Yes. You were the one I was worried about telling. And I realize I didn't do you any favors by keeping it from you. I'm not perfect, sweetie. Can you forgive me for screwing up?"

"Of course, Dad. I don't need you to be perfect. I just need you to be my dad."

Her father squeezed her hand. "I'm really glad we had this talk, Emma. I think it's put us on the right track. And tomorrow we'll all go out for a big Christmas dinner so you can finally get to know Tara a little better."

"Actually, I've been thinking, I'd really like to have our Christmas dinner at home, like we used to."

Her father smiled. "I think that's an excellent idea. We can order in and—"

"No, Dad. I want to cook dinner. It was always our family tradition and it would be nice to share it with Tara and Colin."

Her father's face filled with so much emotion his eyes sparkled. "Tara would absolutely love that. She's been dying to make her family's lasagna recipe. I guess it's what her grandparents used to do for Christmas, but I didn't think you'd be up for that."

"I don't care what we eat, Dad. I just want to spend time together."

"Me too, sweetheart." He squeezed her hand. "Is there anything else that would make your Christmas day special?"

"Do you think it would be okay if Will joined us? His parents aren't home and I don't want him to be alone on Christmas."

Her father tried to school his expression, which had quirked into a smile at the mention of Will. "This might be a shot in the dark, but is Will the boy from your story?"

Emma bit her lip but nodded.

"I know you don't need it, but you have my blessing when it comes to him. He's a good kid. And I know he cares about you deeply. I don't know what he may have done in the past. But sometimes you have to be willing to let it go if you want to have a future."

Emma smiled. "Ya know, you're pretty good at boy talk, Dad."

He laughed. "Well that's a relief. But I'm still praying Tara's having a boy. I don't think my hairline could survive another daughter," he said running a finger through his thinning silver hair.

"Hey!" Emma swatted him and they both laughed.

"I may have one more piece of advice for you," he offered.

"Oh yeah, what's that?"

"Why don't you invite Will to the Christmas Eve party on the rooftop tonight?"

"I told Tara I'd watch Colin while you both went."

"I think it would do us good to go as a family, don't you?"

Emma smiled. "Actually, yeah. I think that's a perfect idea."

Will

WILL WAS PRACTICALLY giddy as he unwrapped the corsage. He was confident with his selection. It was a simple white gardenia with a few pine sprigs. Understated and elegant, just like Emma.

The corsage was much simpler than the holiday themed arrangements the florist had suggested. He'd shivered when the woman tried to hand him one made of pale pink roses and iridescent icicles. It was nearly identical to the one he'd held for hours on the night Emma stood him up. *That's not gonna happen again,* Will told himself. *Not this time.*

Will placed the delicate corsage in his refrigerator and checked his phone again. Still no messages from Emma. He'd sent her one after talking to Tara, saying to text him when she got home. But that had been hours ago. He didn't want to text her again. It seemed too desperate. But he wanted to give her enough time to get ready for the rooftop party. It was a formal affair and he knew she'd need time to get ready. *That is, if she agreed to go with him.*

Emma

WHEN EMMA GOT HOME she glanced at her phone again. The message from Will was taunting her. *Text me when you get home.* She had every intention of doing so, but first there was something she needed to take care of.

Emma knocked on Colin's door, peeking her head in. He

was lying on his bed with Hodor, reading a thick book that looked beyond his years. The scene made her smile.

Colin's face lit up when he saw her. "Hi Emma!"

"Hey buddy, do you have time to help me with a secret mission?"

He sat up. "What kinda mission?"

"One for Will."

"Is it another Christmas gift?"

"No, it's more like an I'm sorry gift."

Colin scrunched up his face. "What are you sorry for?"

"Lots of things, but mostly for not being able to see the future sooner."

"What does that mean?"

Emma sighed. She hadn't expected so many questions. "He'll know what I mean."

"But how?"

"It's a girl thing, just trust me, okay?"

Colin rolled his eyes. "Girls are weird." But then he shrugged. "Okay. I'm in. What do you need me to do?"

Emma grinned. "Do you have any paper?"

36

ill

THERE WAS a knock at Will's front door and he leapt off the couch. *Finally!* He was beginning to think Emma was ignoring him again. But disappointment flooded Will when it wasn't Emma at his door.

"Hey, Colin. What's up?" Will asked trying not to sound dejected.

"This is for you," the little boy replied, thrusting an oddly folded bundle of paper at him.

Will took it and examined the folds as nostalgia flooded him. It was a piece of lined notebook paper folded to look like a small envelope. But in the center there was a tab that read, '*pull me*'. Beneath it a tiny arrow was drawn to indicate the direction. He and Emma used to write notes to each other and fold them that way when they were kids. Emma learned how to do it at summer camp one year and when she'd come home she taught

Will. They spent an entire year exchanging them in their lockers.

He was about to open the note when he realized Colin was still standing there, staring at him expectantly. "Do you need anything else?" Will asked.

"Emma said I need to wait for your response."

"Oh. Okay."

Will pulled the tab. The note unfolded and a silver ticket fell out. He picked it up and read the information printed on it.

Rooftop Garden Gala
To benefit the Manhattan Garden Club
Christmas Eve
The Strathmore Terrace
9 o'clock
Formal attire required

WILL GRINNED. This couldn't be more perfect. He'd been planning to ask Emma to the rooftop party and she was already a step ahead of him. His eyes slid to the note she'd written.

Will, You were right. I'm sorry I didn't see it sooner. But I'm all out of doubts. I know what I want. If your offer still stands, meet me at the rooftop party tonight. – Emma

BELOW HER MESSAGE were three hand drawn boxes, each with a word next to them. *Yes. No. Maybe.* Beneath the boxes was a question.

Do you still believe in mistletoe and miracles?

Will blinked at the paper in disbelief. *Emma was quoting him.* That was the exact phrase he'd used to ask her to the winter formal last year. *That had to be a good sign.* Maybe they could finally put that awful night behind them. Flush with hope, Will took the pen from Colin's outstretched hand without hesitation. His answer was yes. It had always been yes. Will drew a bold checkmark in the box before refolding the paper and handing it back to Colin.

The little boy giggled and gave Will a salute before turning to march down the hall.

"Wait!" Will called after him. "Can you give Emma something for me?" He darted inside to grab the corsage. When he placed it into Colin's little hand he said. "Tell Emma, she's a mind reader, and I'll always believe in mistletoe and miracles."

Emma

Emma had barely managed to rein in her excitement when Colin returned the note from Will, delivering a stunning corsage with it. *He'd been planning to ask her to the rooftop party, too!* It made her heart flutter when they were in sync like this. At times it was like they could read each other's minds. It was something she'd never experienced with anyone other than Will.

Now for the final part of the plan—the dress. Emma needed something fabulous and nothing she'd shoved into her Louis

Vuitton carry-on was up to par. But judging by the wardrobe she'd seen thus far, Emma knew just the person to turn to. She steeled herself as she prepared to knock on Tara's door.

"Come in," Tara replied after Emma knocked.

Emma poked her head into the lavish bedroom Tara shared with her father, surprised it was the only room in the apartment with a pop of color. Tara was sitting in a large wing-backed chair, her feet up on the hot pink satin bedspread. The image made Emma want to giggle. Never in a million years would she have thought her father would sleep in a pink bed.

Tara looked up from the baby book she was reading and greeted Emma with a warm smile. "Hello, honey. Is Colin driving you crazy?"

"No, actually I wanted to ask if I might be able to borrow a dress for the rooftop party tonight now that we're all going? I didn't really bring anything that formal."

Tara sprang to her feet, clapping her hands together. "Of course, honey. My closet is your closet."

Emma was surprise by the genuine kindness in Tara's voice as she pulled Emma into the walk-in closet, chattering excitedly. "I'm sure you didn't know this about me, but I'm an only child and I always wished I had a sister to play dress up and do girly things with. Now I'm not going to be presumptuous and think we'd ever be that close, but I just want you to know that I'm so excited to have a beautiful girl like you in my life, Emma. And I'm really looking forward to getting to know you."

"Um, thanks Tara. That means a lot."

Tara's smile made her already beautiful face glow. "So, dresses," she exclaimed as if she'd forgotten why they were in her closet for a moment. "All my formal attire is over here. And please, help yourself to anything you like. And not just for tonight. You can borrow anything anytime."

"Really?" Emma asked running a finger over the soft leather of a black Hermés handbag.

"Of course! And what size shoe do you wear?" Tara asked opening a mirrored panel to reveal a backlit shoe wall that would've made Carrie Bradshaw swoon.

"I wear size seven," Emma replied, praying for the first time ever that she and Tara had something in common.

"Me too!" Tara squealed. "Oh this is gonna be so much fun! You pick out some dresses, I'll be in charge of shoes!"

37

ill

Will took a deep breath as he rode the elevator to the roof. He was dressed in his Armani tux, the same one he'd worn to the winter formal last year. It gave him an eerie feeling of déjà vu. There was so much riding on tonight and no matter how many calming breaths he took, he couldn't stop his heart from thundering in his chest.

The elevator finally reached its destination and as the doors dinged open, Will blew out the last of his nerves and stepped off with confidence. *Tonight would end in mistletoe and miracles.* He'd accept no other alternative.

Emma

. . .

EMMA STEPPED off the elevator on her father's arm. Tara was on his other and Colin trailed behind them, excitedly rattling off all the plants he hoped to see at the garden party. Emma couldn't help smiling as she watched her father and Tara make their entrance into the party. Her father looked dashing in his tuxedo and Tara was a vision in red by his side. It was definitely her color, and her flowing Versace gown made her pregnancy glow even more prominent. Colin followed them in a tuxedo that matched her father's right down to the plaid red and green bowtie. The sight was so adorable Emma found herself mirroring her father's hopes that Tara was carrying a baby boy as well.

Colin had grown on Emma over the past few days, and the idea of having another little towhead looking up to her was more than appealing. Will was right—having a little brother was amazing. But it shouldn't have surprised her. *Will was right about a lot of things.*

Speaking of Will . . . Emma's breath hitched when she caught sight of him leaning against the bar across the room. He looked like an old Hollywood film star—devastatingly handsome in his midnight blue tuxedo, fitted to perfection. The blue undertones made his sapphire eyes glow and when he winked at Emma she nearly forgot how to walk in the Prada heels she'd borrowed from Tara.

Emma lifted a hand in greeting and Will wasted no time crossing the room to get to her.

"Hey," he said pulling her into a hug, his husky voice close enough that it rumbled through her. "You look stunning."

"You too," she replied breathily.

Will stepped back hitting her with a bemused smirk. "I was going for dashing, but I guess I can work with stunning."

Emma laughed, glad he'd taken the edge off her nerves with a joke.

"Really, Em . . . that dress . . . you look . . ." He shook his head appraisingly while his eyes devoured her.

She blushed. "Most of the credit goes to Monique Lhuillier."

Emma had settled on an emerald green silk ball gown by one of her favorite designers. She was over the moon when she found it in Tara's closet. The floor length gown fit Emma like a glove and the narrow plunging neckline showed off her best assets. The thin mesh screen over the deep V that nearly reached her navel made it acceptably revealing. And the fully tufted skirt made Emma's slim waist appear even tinier.

Will's eyes roved over the peaks and valleys of the gown. "Remind me to thank Miss Lhuillier for that neckline," he remarked looking at Emma in a way that raised the temperature in the room about a hundred degrees.

Emma's cheeks flushed at Will's comment. Seeming to realize he'd let an unfiltered thought slip, Will cleared his throat and changed the subject. "So, do you want to dance?"

"I'd love to."

Will offered Emma his arm and she took it, letting his intoxicating cologne wash over her as she followed him to the dance floor. He wrapped his strong arms around her, letting his hands settle on her lower back. His thumb slowly grazed circles on her skin thanks to the open back of her gown and Emma grinned at him. They were nearly eye-level, thanks to Tara's killer heels. *The perfect kissing height.*

"I'm really glad we're doing this," Will murmured, pulling Emma closer as the jazz trio began to play '*Silver Bells*'.

"Me too."

"Part of me was afraid you wouldn't show," Will admitted.

Emma ducked her head in shame, but Will's gentle fingers found her jaw, tilting her head back up until they were eye-to-eye. "Will, I'm really sorry about everything last year. I just . . . I want to put it behind us. All of it."

"Me too, Em. More than anything." He pulled her corsage-clad hand to his lips and kissed it, sending fire through her veins. "I was really hoping tonight would be a chance to recreate the winter formal we didn't get to have."

"We don't need to recreate anything, Will. Let's just focus on the future."

"Am I in that future?" he asked softly.

Emma pinned him with a look. "I'd like you to be."

He exhaled, pulling her closer. When they were cheek-to-cheek Will pressed his lips to her ear. "You have no idea how much I like the sound of that."

Emma pulled back, her hands sliding from Will's broad shoulders to his chest. She could feel his heart pounding beneath her touch as she gazed into his brilliant blue eyes.

"Em, I've been wanting to tell you how I feel for a long time."

"And how do you feel?" she asked, aware that she was barely breathing as she waited for his response.

"I—"

"There you are, Will," a shrill voice interrupted.

Emma glanced over, locking eyes with none other than Liz Vanderveer. *You've got to be kidding!*

Liz turned her attention to Emma. "Hello, Emmy. Do you mind?" she asked, snaking her claws around Will's arm. "I need to borrow him for family photos."

Emma was already taking a step back in defeat, when Will's grip on her waist tightened, halting her. "Not now, Liz."

"But—"

"I said, not now," Will growled.

Liz took a surprised step backward, her perfectly painted red lips agape. Emma's chest swelled with pride. *Take that Liz. He's picking me!*

Liz regained her composure and gave Will an icy glare. "Fine. I'll let you explain to my mother why you suddenly refuse to take a family portrait." Then she spun on her heel and stalked away.

"I'm sorry about that," Will said, trying to sound calm, but the muscles feathering in his jaw said he was anything but.

Emma blinked at Will in disbelief. She'd never seen him lash out at anyone. It was strangely invigorating. "It's okay," Emma replied, stroking a soothing hand down the strong column of Will's neck.

He leaned into her touch, closing his eyes for a moment. "No, it's not. I know you don't like Liz, but unfortunately my brother saddled us with her forever."

Emma sighed. And there it was. Liz was going to be in Will's life forever. *Could Emma really handle that?* She heard her father's words echo in her mind. '*Sometimes you have to be willing to let it go if you want to have a future.*' And she desperately wanted a future with Will. Emma had allowed herself to glimpse slivers of it over the past few days and now even the thought of letting that go was devastating.

She took a steadying breath. "Will, it's not easy for me knowing you've been with her, but as long as it's in the past—"

Will's posture stiffened. "What did you just say?"

"That I'm willing to move past it as long as whatever was going on with you and Liz is over."

"Me and Liz?" Will raked his hands through is hair looking like he wanted to scream. Instead, he took Emma's hand and silently led her off the dance floor to a quiet corner of the garden rooftop.

He exhaled and regained his composure. "Emma, I don't now how many ways I can say this. There is no me and Liz and there never has been. If you think something otherwise, you need to tell me so we can clear it up right now."

Emma's heart pounded and her dress felt too tight as she struggled to take a proper breath. *This was not how tonight was supposed to go. Not again.* But Emma was determined not to let Liz come between them anymore. "Will it doesn't matter."

"Yes it does, Emma. It matters to me that you believe something that's not true."

A single tear escaped, sliding down her cheek as she felt everything she wanted slipping away.

Will wiped her tear away, pressing his warm hand to her cheek. "Em," he whispered. "I don't think I can handle losing you again."

"Me either."

"Then you gotta talk to me if we're ever gonna have a chance."

She knew he was right. She needed to just get it all out in the open. She'd given her father the abridged version just this morning. *She could do this.*

"Fine." Emma blew out a breath. "I know you were with Liz at Cranston's birthday party before the formal last year."

Will looked confused. "What about it? Half the school was there."

"Well half the school didn't have sex with Liz in Cranston's closet."

Will's face paled and his blue eyes looked like they were going to pop out of his head. "Christ, Emma! Is that what you've thought this whole time?"

"Yes. And it kills me!"

"Emma, I didn't hook up with Liz!"

"Don't, Will! Just please don't make this worse by lying to me."

"I'm not lying," Will bellowed.

"Well someone is, because the photos I saw don't lie."

"What photos?"

Now it was Emma's turn to growl in frustration. "If you weren't the only person at St. James without Snapchat you wouldn't be asking me that question. You can't tell me you haven't seen them. The Lill-ship was practically trending after Cranston's party."

"Em, in English please."

"I'm saying all the proof you need is on Snapchat."

Will crossed his arms defiantly. "Fine, show me the pictures and I'll show you you're wrong, because nothing has ever happened between me and Liz."

"Do you even know how Snapchat works?"

"Let me guess, it shows complete BS?"

Emma narrowed her eyes ignoring his social media dig. "The pictures disappear unless you save them and I didn't care to take screen shots of you and Liz getting it on."

"So you don't have any proof?"

"No."

Will took Emma's hands, his eyes pleading. "Emma, nothing happened with Liz."

Those five little words shattered her heart, because as Emma looked into Will's shining eyes she couldn't detect a hint of dishonesty. But she knew he was lying. She'd seen the pictures. She tried to say as much but was afraid she'd burst into tears and this wasn't the place for a scene.

She turned and tried to walk away, but Will caught her. "Emma, please tell me you believe me."

But she shook her head. "I could have forgiven you. But you can't even admit what you did. How can you ever ask me to believe anything you say?"

"Because it's not true! I've never slept with Liz." Lowering his voice, he added. "I've never slept with anyone."

"Will, I saw the pictures!"

"And you believe them over me?"

"They're photos, Will. What am I supposed to think?"

"Seriously? Have you ever heard of Photoshop, Em? And I don't know, maybe you could have enough faith in your best friend to come to me about this instead of cutting me out of your life."

"I tried. I was walking to your locker the next day to confront you and Liz was there with her arm around your waist. And I just knew it was true."

"So that's why you left? You stood me up at the formal and moved to Boston because of a few photos that may or may not look like me and Liz Vanderveer getting it on?"

"Don't joke about this, Will. You have no idea how embarrassed and hurt I was."

"I'm not joking, Emma. And I think I have a pretty damn good idea how shitty it feels to think someone you love thinks nothing of you."

Will's chest was rising and falling rapidly as he paced a tight line in their quiet corner. Finally he stopped and collected himself. Will reached for Emma's hand, but she pulled away. The hurt expression on his face almost made her reconsider. But her father was wrong—love wasn't worth it. Not if this is what it felt like when it fell apart.

She withdrew another step. "I can't do this, Will."

Will

WILL STOOD WATCHING Emma retreat from their dark corner of the garden in stunned silence. *What the hell just happened?*

One minute he was swaying on the dance floor with Emma in his arm, every dream he'd ever had about to come true; then . . . He didn't even know how to explain what had just happened. But one thing he did know was that it started with Liz. And it was about time he ended it.

Will scanned the party until he spotted Liz. *It was time to get answers.*

38

Emma

EMMA FOUND her father on the dance floor with Tara and Colin. She caught his eye and his face turned stony. "What's wrong, sweetheart?"

"I don't want to talk about it right now, Dad. I just wanted to let you know I'm going back down to the apartment."

"Do you want us to come with you, honey?" Tara asked.

"No, stay and enjoy the party. I just want to be alone right now."

Tara gave her a tight smile and her father nodded, giving Emma a kiss on the cheek. "I'm here if you need me, sweetheart."

"Thanks, Dad." And with that, Emma fled from the dance floor.

She was working her way toward the exit when she felt a

little hand tugging her back. She turned to see Colin dragging his feet as he clung to her wrist. "Emma wait!"

"Hey, buddy. What's wrong?"

"Did your I'm sorry plan with Will work?"

Emma's face fell. "No. It didn't."

"Why not?"

"It's complicated."

"Well you can try again, right? I'll help you tomorrow."

"Thanks, Colin. But I don't think it's going to work."

"But you like Will. And I know Will really likes you. So why can't you just both like each other? Then everyone can be happy and we can have the best Christmas ever."

Colin's little face looked so hopeful it made Emma's heart ache. She knelt down to his level. "Sometimes things aren't that simple, buddy."

He frowned. "But why not?"

How was she supposed to explain this to a seven-year-old? "Things get harder when you're older."

"Maybe that means you have to try harder," Colin offered.

Emma pulled Colin into her arms. The little boy had no idea how right he was. But no matter how hard Emma tried, it seemed nothing short of a miracle could save the future she'd so desperately wanted with Will.

"Emma, look," Colin whispered.

She released him from her hug and trained her eyes to where he was pointing. She nearly gasped when she saw Will shouting heatedly at Liz.

"Whoa! Will looks mad."

Before Emma had time to decide she didn't want to watch their lovers' spat, Will had ripped Liz's phone from her hands and was storming their way, with Liz on his heels. Emma grabbed Colin and pulled him behind a wall of vines to keep Will and Liz from seeing them. But the greenery did nothing to shield Emma from their words.

. . .

Will

WILL THUMBED FURIOUSLY through Liz's iPhone for the photos in question. "Where are they Liz?"

"Will, stop it!"

"Not until you tell me the truth. Where are the pictures Emma's talking about?"

"There aren't any pictures," Liz screeched.

"You're so full of it, Liz. You think I don't know why you're lying?"

"I'm not lying."

"Yes you are! Show me the damn pictures or I'm going to your parents right now and we can have this discussion in front of them."

"Go ahead. I didn't keep the photos. You really think I'm that dumb?"

"So they exist?"

"Maybe."

Will's temper was nearing its boiling point. If Liz were a guy Will would've sucker punched him already. Instead he kept her phone out of reach while scrolling back to last December. And when he got there, his blood ran cold. There they were—shot after shot of Liz and a guy wearing Will's face in scandalous positions. There were dozens of them.

Will rubbed his face, the impact of what these photos must've done to Emma finally hitting him. "Jesus, Liz. This . . . I . . ." he sputtered as he scrolled through the flawlessly edited photos. Even Will himself would've been fooled by the level of perfection in Liz's photos. "How did you do this?"

She shrugged. "I used Snip."

Will just blinked numbly at her.

"It's Marcy's father's plastic surgery app. It's amazing, right?"

Will raked a hand over his face as the aftershocks of the incriminating photos rippled through him. "Why would you do this? I mean, what the hell were you thinking, Liz?"

"That we belong together," Liz replied, slipping her arm through his. "We're meant to be. Just like Hazel and Thomas."

Will shook her off, completely repulsed. "Liz, there's nothing between us and after what you did to Emma, there's not a chance in hell that I'm even going to be your friend."

"Will—"

"No, I'm done, Liz. And you better pray that I can fix things with Emma or I swear to God . . ."

"What are you so mad about? All I did was try to save you from yourself? Are you seriously going to throw away our potential for someone like Emma Rhodes? That family has more issues than Vogue. You're too good for her. You're a Taylor. You belong with someone like me."

"Do you hear yourself, Liz? You're insane. There *is* no us. And if you screwed up my last chance to fix things with Emma, I'll never forgive you."

"Why do you care? She doesn't even live here anymore."

"But she could," Will interjected.

Liz laughed bitterly. "You think she'd move back here for you? Your parents don't even come home to spend time with you."

"This isn't about my parents. This is about me and Emma. And people do crazy things for love all the time."

"Oh, and what, you love her?"

"Yes! I do. I always have. But you took away any chance I had to find out how she feels about me."

Liz looked truly astonished. "You'd throw away what we have for a chance?"

"We don't have anything, Liz! But yes. I'd throw away everything for even just the slightest chance with Emma."

"But—"

"No, Liz. This is over. Leave Emma alone and don't speak to me again." And before he did or said something he couldn't take back, Will stormed away from Liz Vanderveer, praying he would find Emma in time to beg her to forgive him for being the world's biggest idiot.

Emma

EMMA SAT in stunned silence behind the wall of vines, her hands still clutched over Colin's ears. Her heart was hammering so hard she could barely hear anything over it. But when Colin tugged on her arm it pulled Emma back to reality.

"What?" she asked, staring at Colin's grinning face.

"I told you he loves you."

Emma shot to her feet. *He had said that, hadn't he?* In the mix of all the other foul and terrible things Liz had admitted, Will had said the only thing that mattered. *He loved Emma.*

"I have to find him," she whispered more to herself than Colin, but a moment later, both of them were running back toward the party.

39

ill

Will was frantically searching the rooftop for Emma without any luck. He spotted her father and Tara on the dance floor but she was nowhere in sight. He knew she'd probably left. He'd seen the hurt in her eyes when she'd pulled away from him. She was probably in her apartment packing while he wasted time searching the stupid party.

Cursing himself, Will made for the exit only to run smack into Colin. "Hey, Colin. Have you seen your sister?"

"I'm right here."

Will turned at the sound of Emma's voice, relief flooding him to see her again. He rushed toward her, already pleading his case for forgiveness, but all he got out was her name before Emma's lips crashed into his.

Will was so surprised by the kiss that he stumbled back a

step before regaining his balance. His eyes were blown wide as he stared into Emma's. "Em . . ." Will didn't know what to say. He wanted to apologize for everything, but Emma's kiss left him speechless.

"I know," she whispered. "I know what Liz did."

"You do?"

"I heard everything."

Relief flooded through Will in a wave that nearly floored him.

"Oh thank God. Can you ever forgive me, Em?"

She nodded. "There's nothing to forgive."

Will pulled Emma into his arms, crushing her against him like he might fall apart other wise. He never wanted to let her go. He wanted to keep her this close for the rest of his life and the fear of not getting to do that was strangling him. "I'm in love with you," he whispered.

Emma pulled back just enough to look at him. "I love you, too," she said breathlessly.

Will felt the world still, and in that moment there wasn't another soul on that roof top as he slowly brought his lips to Emma's. They met with a brush of heat that felt like fireworks branding his skin. Will slid his hands up Emma's back, wrapping one firmly in her silken hair as he kissed her the way he'd always meant to. Like breathing. Like flying. Like everything good in the world.

Emma

IT HAPPENED QUICKLY, and Emma didn't fight it as her heart let go of all the love she'd been holding back. She curled into the warmth of Will's embrace as the sudden realization washed over her with certainty. She was in love with Will Taylor. Always had been. Always would be.

It had taken them sixteen years of friendship, plus one broken year apart, but they'd found their way back to each other—to where they were meant to be. And as Will kissed her under the starlight winter sky, she knew she was never going to let him go.

WHEN THEIR PUBLIC display of affection started to draw attention, Will wisely drew Emma away from center of the party to a secluded corner where they could sit and talk.

"Em?" he asked, hesitance in his eyes. "Tell me this is real."

She glowed as she answered. "It's real."

Will took her hands in his. "I never stopped missing you. Not for a second."

"Me too. I was just so afraid of getting my heart broken again," she admitted.

"God, I'm so sorry. I feel like such an idiot. I had no idea, Emma. If I had—"

"You couldn't have," she interrupted. "I always knew Liz was evil, but she's clearly insane."

Will groaned, "I still can't quite believe it. I wanted to kill her when I saw the photos."

Emma grinned. "I've gotta say, it sorta turns me on when you get all white knight like that."

"Oh yeah?" Will asked, the mischievous twinkle returning to his blue eyes.

Emma smirked at him. "Yeah."

Will pulled her into his lap and dipped her into a deep, lingering kiss that left her breathless. When he pulled her back up he ran a finger down her cheek and planted a soft kiss on her forehead. "All joking aside, I don't ever want to let a misunderstanding like that come between us again."

"Me either," Emma murmured.

Will exhaled and buried his face into Emma's neck. "God, Em. When I think I might have lost you forever because of some stupid app . . ." He looked up at her suddenly. "I think it's time I get on social media."

Emma laughed. "We don't need social media. We just need to stop being too scared to admit how we feel to each other."

"I think we're off to a pretty good start," he said nuzzling her neck in a way that made her feel faint. "I love you, Emma Rhodes."

She grinned. "I don't think I'll ever get tired of hearing you say that."

"You better not. I'm gonna be saying it for a really long time."

"How long?" she teased.

"I was sorta thinking the rest of my life."

Emma's heart did a series of backflips that left her shaking.

"Is that okay with you?" Will asked, noting her slight tremor.

"Very okay," she said leaning in to kiss him again.

"I don't think I'll ever get tired of that," he teased, breaking from her lips. "Although . . ."

"Although what?"

"It's just funny. This wasn't at all how I envisioned our first kiss."

"How did you picture it?" Emma asked.

"I was sure it would be under the mistletoe," he said nodding to boughs that hung over the dance floor.

"Well in the spirit of making dreams come true, I'm willing to have a first kiss do over with you, Will Taylor."

. . .

Will

WILL TWIRLED Emma onto the dance floor. Her laughter filled his heart near bursting. The band struck up '*Have Yourself A Merry Little Christmas*' and Will pulled Emma into his arms. They swayed back and forth under the strands of white lights and stars. Closer and closer they crept to the center of the dance floor, where the mistletoe danced above them suspended on strands of white lights, as if they were hung from the stars.

When they were perfectly centered below the mistletoe, Will took Emma in his arms, pulling her near. He traced his hand down the smooth curve of her face, stopping when he reached her pale pink lips.

"Emma Rhodes, you are why I believe in mistletoe and miracles."

And then he kissed her.

Emma sighed into his mouth, meeting his lips with a tenderness that filled even the deepest aches of his heart.

They danced under the starlight and mistletoe, stealing kisses and indulgent glances until Will felt a tug at his sleeve. He looked down to see Colin grinning up at them, with Tara and Emma's father watching from a distance.

"What's up, Colin?" Emma asked smiling down at the little boy.

"Everything worked out, didn't it?"

Emma beamed. "Yeah, it did."

Colin's grin spread even wider. "I told you he loved you."

Will barked a laugh. "I didn't know the secret was out."

Colin shrugged. "Oh and just so you know, mistletoe isn't for high-fives." His little voice dropped to a whisper. "It's for kissing."

Will glanced at Emma, both of them raising their eyes to

the merry green sprigs bobbing above their heads. Will could barely take a breath, his chest tight with wild joy as Emma raised her face to his, dropping a tender kiss on his lips.

Colin giggled then turned to run back to Tara and Emma's father, who waved their goodnights from across the dance floor.

40

Emma

WILL HELD Emma in his arms all night, as they danced under the stars. She could've stayed there with him forever, content to live in that moment with him gazing at her like she was the only girl in the world. But as the band announced their last song, Emma felt the cold grip of reality seep in, biting at the bliss she found in Will's adoring eyes.

As if sensing it, Will asked, "What are you thinking?"

"I'm thinking I wish tonight didn't have to end."

He grinned. "Me too."

"I just wish we could get last year back. We wasted so much time."

Will met her eyes. "Maybe, or maybe we were just meant to be together right now. Right here. In this moment."

"But I don't want this moment to end."

"Maybe it doesn't have to," he said, his eyes clear and bright. "Come on."

Will

Will led Emma off the dance floor and to his apartment. He refused to even let her leave his side long enough to go to her father's and change. Instead he gave her his lacrosse jersey and a pair of tall wool socks that stretched all the way to her knees. And somehow, when she came out of his bedroom wearing only those items, she looked even sexier than she had in the expensive designer gown.

Will pushed back his aching desires for Emma and led her over to the Christmas tree, where he'd laid out a blanket and pillows.

When she saw it she squealed with delight. "You remembered!"

"Like I could forget our oldest tradition."

Emma beamed at him for a moment before stretching out on the blanket. She lay on her back with her head under the tree so she could gaze up at the lights. She stuck a hand out, wiggling her fingers in invitation for Will to join her. So he crawled under the tree, joining Emma beneath the glowing lights, and slipped his fingers between hers.

For some reason, Emma used to do this to every Christmas tree she saw when she was little. Even in department stores, much to her mother's chagrin. So in an act of solidarity, Will did the same and their tree gazing tradition was born.

This time, laying side-by-side beneath the tree, with Emma's hand in his, things felt much more intimate. And Will realized it was because he finally had everything he'd ever wanted out of life. He had Emma and he could see their future taking shape. He turned to her. “Em, thank you for saving this holiday.” He laughed softly. “And this whole year really.”

“I should be thanking you.”

“What do you mean?”

“I haven’t even had a chance to tell you about my day with my father.”

Will turned on his side and laid his head on his arm to gaze at Emma. His whole face was aglow with happiness. “Tell me.”

And she did, right down to every detail about her new bedroom and design studio, and how Will had been right all along, her father never stopped caring about her. “And the best part is, we’re all staying home to cook a lasagna for Christmas dinner tomorrow and you’re invited.”

Will barked a laugh.

Emma looked at him in wonder. “What?”

“Your father probably dropped a cool mill on your accommodations at his new place and the thing you’re most excited about is cooking lasagna for Christmas?”

“So?”

“Man did I pick the right girl,” he said tugging her close enough to drop a chaste kiss on her lips.

But Emma had other ideas. She deepened their kiss, and every bit of Will’s focus narrowed to the way her body felt pressed against his. Her touch was smoldering embers against his skin, awakening his ache to caress every part of her.

They lay entangled under the tree kissing for a blissful moment longer until Emma pulled away, leaving Will panting with desire.

“Wait,” she said breathlessly. “I thought we came down here to continue our conversation?”

“I was liking the conversation we were having just fine.”

Emma laughed, letting Will pepper her neck with kisses. “Will, I’m serious. What does all this mean?”

"What do you want it to mean?" he asked pulling her against him.

She picked at the button of his dress shirt, nervously. "I leave the day after tomorrow to go back to Boston."

Will sighed. "Well, Boston is only a train ride away. I can visit."

She looked up at him optimistically. "You'd come visit?"

"Every weekend if you want. Hell I'd move there if you wanted me to."

She grinned, kissing him again. "Maybe I could come here some weekends too," she offered. "And I'm gonna need a date for my father's wedding . . ."

"I think I could handle that," Will said, kissing her again. "Although if it was up to me, I'd never let you go."

"I don't want to go," Emma whispered. "I feel like I just got you back."

The sadness in her voice was enough to break Will's heart. "Hey," he said, smoothing her hair. "You never lost me, Em. And you never will. School's over in less than six months. And after that nothing can keep us apart."

Emma sighed into Will's chest. "You're right. This is going to work."

Will kissed the top of her head and pulled her closer. "It has to."

41

Emma

Emma didn't know how long she and Will laid under the tree holding onto each other, afraid to let go of what they'd finally found. But when she blinked her eyes open, she was in a bed. She sat up. *It was Will's bed.* But he wasn't in it.

She glanced around his room rubbing the sleep out of her eyes. She found Will fast asleep on the soft leather couch in his room. Emma's heart swelled at the sight of him fast asleep. He was still partially sitting up, like he'd fallen asleep watching over her. *Her white knight.*

Emma couldn't wait to spend more morning's waking up with him. And that thought hatched an idea. She slipped silently from the bed and out of Will's apartment, dashing back to her own. She grabbed what she needed and was in and out before anyone even knew she was there. A few minutes later, gift in hand, Emma climbed carefully onto the couch with Will, nestling under the soft duvet with him.

She hadn't realized he was shirtless until she slid under the light blanket he'd draped over himself, but the warm smooth muscles of his chest were a welcome surprise. She cuddled up to him, planting a soft kiss on his stubbly chin. Will made a delicious sound between a growl and a purr and Emma's toes curled. He slid his eyes open for a moment and grinned as he wrapped his arms around her.

"Good morning," she greeted.

"If this is a dream, I can certainly get used to it," Will murmured, his rough morning voice reverberating through her.

She giggled. "It's not a dream. I'm really here. And it's Christmas morning," she whispered, looking up at him.

"This is the best dream ever," Will replied planting a kiss atop her bedroom hair.

She grinned at his adorableness, but continued to prod him. "Will, wake up. I want to give you your Christmas present."

Emma felt him smile into her hair. "God, I love this holiday."

"Not that!" she said, playfully swatting him. "Here," she said shoving an envelope into his hands.

Will

Will sat up, pulling Emma with him. "What's this?" he asked examining the unmarked envelope.

"Open it."

Emma watched him with blatant glee, making Will want to take his time opening the gift just to prolong that look on her beautiful face. But when he pulled out the folded page of printed paper inside he started to shake with laughter.

"What's so funny?" Emma asked, her prior amusement dissolving.

"Give me a sec," he said sliding off the couch. He crossed the room and grabbed a thin white tie box from his desk and brought it back to Emma. She took it from him cautiously as he climbed under the blankets next to her.

"Open it," he said, watching her trepidation while trying to conceal his smirk.

Emma pulled the top off the white box to reveal three rows of wintermint Tic Tacs. She looked at him without amusement. "Tic Tacs?"

"The real gift is underneath."

Emma dumped the candy onto her lap revealing a piece of printed paper nearly identical to the one she'd given him. Only the departure and arrival cities were reversed.

Emma flipped the train ticket over in awe, reading the words he'd written on the backside.

Will said them out loud just for good measure. "We'll always have mistletoe and miracles."

Emma threw her arms around his neck, half sobbing and laughing at the same time. "How did it ever take us this long to get together? I mean we bought each other the same gift."

"Train tickets are a hot item this season," Will joked.

"We're gonna be okay," Emma whispered.

Will found himself still smiling as the coiled feeling in his chest began to loosen. "Absolutely."

Emma grinned. "I love you, Will. Merry Christmas."

"Merry Christmas, my love."

EPILOGUE

ill

After a little more celebrating in his bedroom, Will joined Emma and her family for the best family Christmas he'd ever had. Everyone thanked Will for the beautiful live tree he'd snuck into their apartment during the wee hours of Christmas morning. And between watching Colin open presents under the live tree and spending the day with Emma's family cooking lasagna and Christmas cookies, Will felt he was living a dream.

The highlights of the day were when Tara gave Teddy an ultrasound in a tiny blue picture frame that read, '*It's a Boy!*' Colin had been so excited by the idea of having a little brother, he immediately started going through all his toys to pick out which ones he wanted to give to the baby. When Tara finally convinced him that he had a few months to figure all that out, Teddy called everyone to the living room so he could share his gift.

He played a slide show on the television showing photos of the new home they'd be moving into on New Year's day, and Tara about fainted. In all the commotion no one noticed Hodor sneak into the kitchen to eat the rest of the lasagna they'd left on the counter. But of course his trail of tomato sauce footprints gave him away.

When everything had settled down, Will proved to have one last surprise up his sleeve by queing up a film he'd made for Emma titled, '*Our First Christmas.*'

"Someone was confident," Emma teased snuggling closer to him on the couch.

"I prefer, optimistic," Will replied, unashamed.

Emma giggled as everyone swooned over the adorable candid shots Will had complied over the last few days they'd spent together. To Colin's delight, the film even included clips of him from their trips to Central Park and Emmerich Tree Farm.

But the icing on the proverbial fruitcake had come when Emma stood up after Will's film to announce that she was moving back to New York after graduation. Will was practically in tears. And as everyone gathered Emma in a massive family hug, Colin exclaimed. "This is the best Christmas ever."

Will didn't think his life could get any better. Somehow, both Colin and Emma's Christmas wishes had come true. And along with it, all of Will's wildest dreams.

Emma

As the night drew to a close, Emma kissed Tara, Colin and her father goodnight and walked back to Will's to spend her last night in New York—until she cashed in her train ticket, of course.

They had just settled on his couch to gaze at the Christmas tree, determined to stay awake as long as possible and make the most of their time together when a notification on Emma's phone dinged. She looked at it and jumped up in alarm.

"What's wrong?" Will asked.

"Nothing. But can I borrow your laptop really fast?"

"Of course."

Emma was already running to Will's room. She had ten minutes to revise her post before it went live. She pulled up her blog and deleted everything she'd written on her way to New York. Then she started typing. With three minutes to spare, Emma was finally satisfied with her post and hit submit. She smiled at the bullet points under the post heading. And she didn't stop smiling until she was kissing the boy they were all about.

A Haute Chic's Holiday Survival Guide

1. *Family is everything.*
2. *Falling in love is worth it.*
3. *You're never too old to believe in mistletoe and miracles.*

ALSO BY CHRISTINA BENJAMIN

YOUNG ADULT CONTEMPORARY ROMANCE

(All Boyfriend Books are Stand-Alone Novels and can be read in Any Order)

The Practice Boyfriend (Book 1)

The Almost Boyfriend (Book 2)

The Goodbye Boyfriend (Book 3)

The Holiday Boyfriend (Book 4)

The Stand-In Boyfriend (Book 5)

The Maybe Boyfriend (Book 6)

The Accidental Boyfriend (Book 7)

The Summer Boyfriend (Book 8)

The Wedding Boyfriend (Book 9)

The Winter Boyfriend (Book 10)

To my readers,

I want to personally thank you for taking the time to seek out this great little indie book. Writing is truly my passion. I believe each of us can find a small part of ourselves in every book we read, and carry it with us, shaping our world, our adventures and our dreams.

Following my dream to write frees my soul but knowing others find joy in my writing is indescribable. So thank you for your support and I hope your enjoyed your brief escape into the magic of these pages.

If you enjoyed this story, don't worry, there's plenty more currently rattling around in my rambunctious imagination. Let me and others know your thoughts by sharing a review of this book. Reviews help shape my next writing projects. So if you want more books like this one be sure to shout it from the rooftops (or social media) ;-)

ABOUT THE AUTHOR

Award-Winning author, Christina Benjamin, lives in Florida with her husband, and character inspiring pets, where she spends her free time working on her books and enjoying a macaron with a glass of wine.

Christina is best known for her bestselling Young Adult romance novels, The Boyfriend series. The Boyfriend series proves that book boyfriends are like Chocolate… you can never have enough. Check out the Boyfriend series for fast, fun, YA romance reads. These stand alone novels let you fall in love with new characters every time.

Want to talk books with Christina? Join her super secret Facebook group Words & Wine with Christina Benjamin, where she'll answer questions and discuss upcoming novels with her readers.

To learn about new books and more fun stuff, follow her at:

FACEBOOK
@ChristinaBenjaminAuthor

TWITTER
@authorcbenjamin

INSTAGRAM
@authorcbenjamin

PINTEREST
@authorcbenjamin

WEBSITE
www.christinabenjaminauthor.com

www.ingramcontent.com/pod-product-compliance
Lightning Source LLC
Chambersburg PA
CBHW030529310726
48979CB00010B/1845/J
* 9 7 8 1 7 3 2 6 1 2 3 3 4 *